YANQUI  A

# YANQUI

## Tom W. Blackburn

Chivers Press • G.K. Hall & Co.
Bath, England   Thorndike, Maine USA

This Large Print edition is published by Chivers Press, England, and by G.K. Hall & Co., USA.

Published in 1998 in the U.K. by arrangement with Golden West Literary Agency.

Published in 1998 in the U.S. by arrangement with Golden West Literary Agency.

U.K. Hardcover ISBN 0–7540–3126–8 (Chivers Large Print)
U.S. Softcover ISBN 0–7838–8292–0 (Nightingale Collection Edition)

The text of this Large Print edition is unabridged.
Other aspects of the book may vary from the original edition.

Set in 16 pt. New Times Roman.

Printed in Great Britain on acid-free paper.

**British Library Cataloguing in Publication Data available**

**Library of Congress Cataloging-in-Publication Data**

Blackburn, Thomas Wakefield.
    Yanqui / Tom W. Blackburn.
        p.   cm.
    ISBN 0–7838–8292–0 (large print : sc : alk. paper)
    1. Large type books.   I. Title.
[PS3552.L3422Y36   1998]
813′.54—dc21                                          97–35651

*For*
*E. W. Alsdorf*
*'BABE'*
*Who reads them all*

# PROLOGUE

There is something unique about the Southwest that makes it the brightest warp in the many-colored pattern of frontier history, and it is this: here men did not make the land; the land made men. Nowhere is this more true than in the high country of New Mexico.

The ball of a man's thumb, placed on a map of the north-central portion of the present state at the eastern base of the Sangre de Cristo mountains, would cover an area about the size and shape of the Corona Grant. The Corona occupied a valley—more properly a great basin containing a whole complex of valleys, arroyos, mesas, and buttes—extending along the foot of the mountains for more than a day's ride and reaching a width of perhaps thirty miles.

Beyond it to the east lay a sea of grass, sloping off imperceptibly into the monotonous aridity of the *Llanos estacados*, the Staked Plains of the Texas Panhandle. The Corona was high—more than six thousand feet at the spot where its founder built the great house for his wife over the years—and from its western rim vistas extended over a hundred miles.

Most of the Corona was richly grown with various chaparral and thick-sodded grama grasses, but its watered bottoms were dotted

1

with cottonwood and willow and its mountain rim rose to summer snow above alpine aspen and jackpine. The symmetrical cinder cone, set quite apart on the south and known as Fire Mountain, was the boundary of the malpais, an almost impenetrable badlands area of narrow canyons and massy, tumbled lava, spewed from Fire Mountain in some cataclysm of the geologic past.

Northward, extending across virtually the whole of the horizon in that direction, was a vast basaltic mesa, high enough to carry snow through most normal winters. This was known as The Reef—and reef it effectually was, protecting the Corona from blizzards that swept, otherwise unchecked, down across the Great Plains. The Crossing, a difficult natural trail, was the only practicable pass over The Reef.

As grassland basins go—even in this richest of all grazing areas—the Corona was indeed the 'Crown' of them all, with living forage in the high valleys and on the upper benches in spring and summer and the self-cured natural hay of the grama on protected bottoms in winter. It was this unfailing year-round graze that, together with its unique geographic isolation, gave the Corona its long and turbulent history.

Indians prized the plentiful game and easy foot hunting in the basin long before the coming of the horse. Apache, Ute, Comanche—in the days of the horse tribes—

fought many battles for the buffalo that ranged there. And in time a great trade highway skirted this incomparable stronghold. From the veranda of the massive main house it is still possible today to trace with a good glass the deep ruts of the Santa Fe Trail for more than twenty miles across the undulating grass to the east.

It was from the east, along this trail, that the first Stanton approached the basin.

# CHAPTER ONE

Stanton slid from his blankets and tugged on his boots, which, with his hat and jacket, constituted dressing. There was a twinge of stiffness in a joint or two. Six hundred miles out from Westport Landing into this Mexican wilderness and more than two thousand miles from the eastern seaboard had not yet won him comfortable peace with hard bedding-grounds and the thin chill of these high false dawns. Time was not kindly in this regard.

As Bolo, his giant Carib Indian overseer often used to say, in time a man's body did not harden as readily as in youth. In time only his determination did. This, the great brown man always insisted, was the real maker of revolutionaries and martyrs and great rascals. They all were seldom very young. Time gave a man that kind of strength.

Stanton hoped this was so. He had come a long way to make a new beginning.

This dry, purple-gray land was not the rich tidewater valleys of Virginia. It was not a planter's country, but he had not been a planter. Neither was it a stockman's country, as he knew stock. But a man could learn. Whatever could be made to thrive here would have to possess the toughness of the country itself. Most important, there was space. With

5

enough space a man could cast a long shadow.

He sucked appreciatively at the morning air. This was his hour. It always had been. Before the true coming of the sun. At this hour the day did not burst upon a man full-blown, forcing him to leap abreast of it at first breath. It came upon him gently, as the blood quickened and the light grew, opening up the horizon and bringing detail into focus as the awakening mind opened and focused. There was time to adjust precisely to full awareness and to step easily into the harmony of routine.

He moved to the water-butt at the near sideboard of his merchandise-laden wagon. As he attended to the brief toilette allowable in a dry camp, the irregular string of freighters tumbled protestingly awake and to first chores in the usual grumbling disorder. Stanton scowled. Discipline had been nonexistent in the train since the first day on the trail. His gaunted, sore-footed beeves, now lowing their own protest out on the dry grass, were more tractable than the men who daily cursed their slowness.

Stanton had no patience with mismanagement of either men or beasts and no qualms about so stating when need be. He had felt the need frequently since he had joined this train and he had won few friends since leaving the river.

Bennett Royer came back along the big freighter hubs on some errand of responsibility. He was accompanied as usual by a gaggle of hangers-on, hired drovers and roust-abouts, without whom the wagonmaster seemed unable to support his burden of authority, such as it was. Stanton did not like the man, an opportunist signed on by an accident of availability for the sole purpose of transporting himself to Santa Fe. He was shrewd enough, powerful and handsome in an arresting brute way, but he was coarse and uneducated and his bullying tactics did little to improve morale. He ran the string as a stray wolf would a pack of dogs.

As Royer came abreast of Stanton's wagon, a youngster, hardly more than a boy, whom Royer had made his personal slave on the first day, came running up on the double with the wagonmaster's first mount of the day. Royer cuffed the boy away when he started to turn the stirrup for him to mount, then swung up unaided. The horse was young, restive, and intent on venting three farts and a whinny to start the day. It crow-hopped a couple of jumps and side-stepped in elaborate, snorting avoidance of an imaginary hazard underfoot. Caught momentarily off-balance before he could fully seat himself, Royer was slammed back onto the cantle rim and then hard forward against the pommel. Only a miracle kept him from being loosened completely and ignominiously hitting the dirt. It was a familiar enough morning mischance to any horseman,

7

who usually laughed off his own inadvertance, but Royer was furious.

Getting his butt in place, he jerked savagely back and forth on the reins, leaning his full weight and power into it. Trail horses were seldom long in acquiring tough mouths, but Royer's anger brought blood at once. The horse danced backward, neighing shrill outrage and trying to escape the punishing bit. Stanton was nearly pinned against his wagon, and the blankets of his bed were trodden into the dust.

Regaining his balance, Stanton caught one of Royer's sawing elbows and jerked him clear of the saddle, swinging him around and slamming him back hard against the wagon wheel. Stanton's toe hooked at his trampled bed.

'You damned fool!' he said harshly. 'Shake out those blankets and stow them in the wagon.'

Without giving the shaken man time to respond or his companions a chance to close up, Stanton caught up the trembling horse and led it back to the startled boy who had brought it up.

'Water this broom-tail and turn it back into the herd,' he ordered. 'Bring another up for the captain. A real razorback, this time, if you can find one.'

The boy looked about uncertainly. All motion within earshot had come to an

8

expectant standstill. The boy caught the relish of anticipation. He sucked himself up straight, grinned self-consciously, and trotted off importantly with the horse. Stanton returned to his wagon.

Royer watched his approach darkly. Hagen, a tall, lank bull-whacker, had moved up beside the wagonmaster, blandly buying in chips for whatever they were worth. Somebody had retrieved Stanton's blankets. They were neatly folded over Hagen's arm. Royer's other cronies, three or four, eased up behind, waiting. Royer was breathing heavily, but he took care to speak softly, so that his words would not carry beyond the immediate group.

'All right, Virginia. We can all be gentlemen, if you so damned well got to have it that way. I'll say it. Sorry. You're going to be, too.'

He waited truculently, eyes probing hopefully for hostile response. With the first flash of his own instinctive anger past, Stanton would have dropped it. He could do well enough without friends in this company, but he didn't especially need enemies.

'Trail fever, Royer,' he said quietly. 'Both of us. You're right. I'm sorry, too.'

'Hell, you don't get off that easy,' Royer growled. 'Not in front of the whole damned train. I'm going to have your balls, mister.'

'We're all risking a gelding if this train doesn't tighten up.'

'Oh, Christ, how many times have I heard

9

that crap before!'

'Every day since we crossed the Canadian,' Stanton admitted. 'Every day on into Santa Fe, if you keep on refusing to listen. We weren't warned up there just to make the rest of the haul exciting. There are Utes in those mountains west of us.'

'Seen any?'

'We will. Common sense. They're human. Our loose stock has got to be to them what black underlace on a woman is to a drover— just too damned fetching not to try lifting. For the hell of it, if nothing else.'

'Bullshit!' Royer snorted. 'Thirty-four wagons with drivers, drovers, and outriders? Sure they're human. And smart. Too smart to tackle anything our size.'

'I could make a dent with a dozen, the way we string out every day.'

Royer glanced at his companions and let his voice out deliberately, so any one who could might hear.

'You son of a bitch, you listen. You listen good. You're one man. One trouble-making bastard. One wagon and a hell of a lot less than the hundred head of worthless cattle you started out with. You and your damned stock have given us fits at every camp and crossing we've hit. I don't care how much you paid at the river to tag them along, we're ten days behind schedule because of you.

'There's traders with ten rigs and a fortune in

10

trade goods in this train. Their reps are no spooked virgins to this trail. Time is money to them. I've heard all hell about the time we're making, but when one of them bellyaches about the way I'm running this string, I'll listen. Till then, I'm shutting you up.'

Royer came at him. Neither was armed at this hour. Stanton knew the folly of letting the big man close in or allowing the others to encircle them, hampering his own movements. He would have avoided this if he could, but he was not displeased. He took the first looping swing on his shoulder. It shook him more than he expected, but he side-stepped, turning Royer, and struck three times—short, hard, and fast—between the ribs and the belt, caving in the lower lungs and driving abdominal organs back against the kidneys.

The wagonmaster doubled up and went down on his side, legs pumping spasmodically with hurt. He rolled slowly over, face into the dirt, and jacked his knees under him. He came up just as slowly, literally lifting himself, shock receding and wind returning. A bystander retrieved his hat and handed it to him. He pulled it on and walked unsteadily away without looking back, still bending a little over his belt.

Silence hung over the camp for a moment. Stanton could again hear the lowing of his beeves. Then, as Royer approached other onlookers, activity hastily resumed. Hagen

11

and the little group with him lingered at Stanton's wagon. Hagen extended the retrieved blankets. Stanton took them.

'Thanks.'

'Your orders, weren't they?' Hagen said. He looked off after Bennett Royer. 'You always got to prod a gored bull?'

Stanton stepped without answer onto a wheel hub and tossed the blankets back in under the tilt. As he dropped to the ground again, Hagen was looking at the big-wheeled, broad-tired, heavily laden freight wagon.

'Any idea what this rig and cargo's worth?' he asked.

'In Sante Fe?'

Hagen shook his head.

'Here.'

'My life,' Stanton said.

'Something to think about, ain't it?'

Hagen smiled, nodded to his companions, and moved off with them. Stanton resumed his chores.

Somewhere down the line the boy brought Royer his replacement mount, and he swung up, bawling orders as he disappeared among the dusty wagon tilts. Camp-break swung into full tide. Breakfast was hastily made at appointed fires and as hastily eaten. Spans of draft animals were brought up, stepped over tongues, and backed in. Trace chains were snapped. Stanton checked his unwatered cattle and found them all up on their feet. He knew

12

some might not last till nightfall, but they would trail as far as they could in hope of water.

In a little more than thirty minutes from the time Stanton had slid from his blankets, just as the first sun crested the eastern horizon, the signal came relaying down the line. Dust sifted up from straining hoofs and broad iron tires, rising chokingly as heavy wheels began to turn.

Stanton lifted the kerchief about his neck to cover mouth and nose and settled back on the spring clip-on seat on the foreboard of his wagon, driving from the right side of the big box to give his whip room to swing. The train strung out as raggedly as usual, so nothing had been accomplished. It was still a long road to Santa Fe.

*       *       *

Two hours later, with the low rise above their dry camp still in sight behind the wagons, the Indians struck. They chose a place where an encroaching arroyo pressed close to the steep slope of a truncated mesa, forcing the trail into a passage too narrow to turn a wagon.

Stanton knew they were the Utes, against whom they had been warned at the crossing of the Canadian. Because of the substantial size of the train, about which Royer had boasted, he assumed the attack would be a quick hit-and-run affair, aimed at the saddle stock

13

trailing the wagons ahead of his beeves. But the Utes employed another tactic.

They came down over the crest of the mesa and up out of the restricting arroyo, converging from both sides on the advance outriders and the lead wagons. The alarmed outriders automatically fell back on the lead wagon, blocking its way in the confusion of surprise and effectively halting the entire train. More horsemen were racing forward, abandoning their assigned wagon segments without orders in hope of relieving the long boredom of the trail with a sporting shot at bow-and-arrow range.

The narrow space between the foot of the mesa and the arroyo quickly choked up, blocking further passage to those coming up from behind. Stanton could not see clearly as dust billowed higher, but there was heavy defensive firing. Too heavy to sustain in such close quarters and still have time to reload.

Yipping war-cries sounded and arrows arched in flat, wicked trajectories, but Stanton did not think there were as many of either as the confusion created by the Indians indicated. He pulled up his spans as tightly as practicable to the wagon ahead. Wrapping his reins in a quick hitch about the brake lever, he snaked his half-stocked new Henry rifle from its embroidered scabbard and ran to his saddled horse at his own tailboard.

He had just dropped his stirrups from the

pommel and was swinging up when Bennett Royer passed at full lope from the tail of the string, where the attack had caught him. The rear-guard outriders were strung out behind him. The mistake was obvious, but Stanton knew the impossibility of overtaking Royer or convincing him in time. Driving his horse among the last of the passing riders, shouting for their attention, he succeeded in diverting a few, who wheeled in behind him, reversing their direction. A few more men along the string found horses and joined them as they passed. They rode back hard for the stock herd, but it was already too late.

The Ute plan had the perfection of simplicity. As Stanton feared, the engagement at the head of the train had been strictly a diversion. The main Indian party—no more than half again the dozen Stanton had wryly suggested in his dawn altercation with Royer— had emerged from the screening arroyo abreast of the milling and now undefended loose stock.

The Utes were audacious and consummate thieves. Each went for one specific horse, no more, ignoring Stanton's bawling beeves. Each cut his prize swiftly from the herd and hazed it at top speed back toward the arroyo, keeping apart from the other Indians so as not to offer a target. With so few driven animals, they moved as freely and fast as if unburdened. And they had the wide advantage of a clean start.

Before Stanton and his party were within

possible range, a heavy gun roared behind him. He chilled and jerked about in his saddle as he felt the heavy slug pass within inches of his body. Hagen was the next man back. Smoke was curling from the muzzle of his rifle. He waved deprecatingly and did not attempt to reload, as though sheepishly recognizing the futility of another shot at the Indians at such distance.

Stanton promised himself words with the freighter at first opportunity. Only a damned fool shot past others of his own party at a full lope. He held on hard for another quarter of a mile and then reined suddenly aside, pulling to an abrupt, sliding stop. Those behind hurtled past and he had a clear angle to the Indians. The first of them reached the rim of the arroyo and dropped from sight with their stolen horses. He was aware that gunfire at the head of the train had suddenly slackened, indicating that the Utes there were also making good their retreat. He thought the missing stock was gone without recourse, but the raiders could not be let off scot-free, if only on general principles.

He flung up the Henry rifle and, from his motionless saddle, swept the horizon until the rearmost of the fleeing Utes floated into silhouette above the front bead. He increased elevation and gently firmed his grip. The rifle fired. The Indian pony went down. Its rider was thrown hard and lay inert. Stanton felt satisfaction. Even in a new beginning, there were some things a man did not have to relearn.

Hagen was among the first to the downed Ute. The Indian was only stunned. When Stanton reached them, Hagen had taken the Ute's knife and had him on his feet, arms twisted up in painful helplessness into the small of his back. He was only a boy, frightened but pridefully defiant.

In the distance another of the raiders reappeared on the rim of the arroyo, disdainfully exposing himself to watch the fate of his comrade. Bennett Royer hammered up with the others from the head of the string. He grinned satisfaction at the captured Ute.

'Stake him out,' he ordered Hagen. 'We'll give the sneaking red bastards a lesson they won't forget.'

'If you want those horses, that boy's the only way you'll get them,' Stanton protested.

'Stake him out,' Royer repeated.

Stanton looked at the arrogant lone raider on the lip of the arroyo. He thrust his discharged rifle under a stirrup leather for freer movement and drew his Navy Colt from its stiff, new holster, lining it on Royer at full cock.

'This time, you listen,' he said. 'No doubt you can carve this youngster into something pretty nasty for his relatives to find when they come back for his body, but what's to be gained? They're traders as well as thieves. He's

17

worth more than a few horses to them.'

Keeping Royer covered, Stanton glanced at the others for some sign of support. To his surprise he saw that Hagen was looking at him with interest and had slackened the painful grip in which he held the young Ute.

'Give me the boy and a couple of men,' Stanton continued to Royer, 'and I guarantee we'll get back the horses.'

Suddenly, as though making up his mind, Hagen completely freed their captive. Young as he was, the boy was wise enough in the ways of men and war to realize the effectiveness of Stanton's pistol. He grasped that for the moment it guaranteed his own safety and so made an instant choice. He darted to Stanton's stirrup, pressed his back against Stanton's knee, and defiantly faced the others from the shadow of the gun above him.

'Virginia's right, Ben,' Hagen said to Royer. 'Look—'

He pointed to the rim of the arroyo and the Ute warrior who had turned back to expose himself there when the boy went down.

'Unless I miss my guess,' Hagen continued, 'that's this one's brother or old man or something. They want him, all right. If there's just a few of us, I think they'll let us come up. I'd say we can make a trade.'

Royer hesitated. Finally he shrugged.

'All right, try it,' he said, deliberately speaking to Hagen rather than Stanton. 'You

18

and Brock. That's enough. But we won't wait. Rest of you, back to the string.' He rode close to Stanton in passing. 'I'll put a man on your wagon. But do me a favor: don't come back.'

Hagen and Brock caught up a loose horse on the edge of the reshaping herd and brought it back. The young Ute mounted without surcingle or halter, fought gently for control for a moment, and rode to Stanton. They started together for the arroyo, Hagen and Brock trailing.

Seeing them coming, the Ute on the rim of the arroyo disappeared. They presently dipped into the wash and found it empty. Stanton began to fear they had gone after all, or were setting another ambush. But at the next turn they were waiting, about thirty of them, with the stolen horses bunched in their midst.

Stanton looked at the young Ute beside him. Both smiled. With that smile on his face, his attention upon the waiting Indians, Stanton was struck in the back by a bullet fired at close range.

He saw the red earth coming up and was swallowed by it.


## CHAPTER TWO

Stanton was troubled by a persistent, recurring dream: that he lay abed with the warm body of

19

a woman. It was different with each awakening, but always the same woman. Waves of delirium, in which spectres stalked, and she drove them away. Waves of icy chill, and her warmth flowed into him. Waves of raging fever, and her body was cool against his, drawing out the fire. Long black places, with no recollection between.

The dream troubled, but Stanton relished the fantasies. They were natural enough, he supposed. How long had it been since he had actually slept in the same bed with a woman? Thirty months since he had moved out of the master's suite at Stanton Hall. Thirty months since he had felt Belle's belly beside him and heard her boast the swelling was with another man's child, a bastard she was carrying to be raised with the two sons he had of her. Thirty months to arrange his affairs. A lifetime and a fortune ago.

He heard voices. They spoke the Spanish he had found no occasion to use since Bolo, the Carib, had spat at his feet and walked away because the brown man would no longer work for a boss who would not fight back. He heard the voices and he felt the hands, insistent, prodding, shaking at him.

'We must waken him, Chato,' one said anxiously. 'It has already been too many days. He must have food and water or he will keep on growing weaker and die.'

'He will die if the wounds reopen, too,' the

second voice answered in a more imperfect Spanish.

'We must take the chance,' the first voice said insistently.

'I am not so sure, 'Mana. This gift of healing—did the gods—your Black Robe God—give it to you?'

'Better than that. I learned it from a book. Here, help me—'

The hands lifted. They hurt like hell. Stanton was forced to open his eyes. He lay on a stretcher-like brush or sapling cot with an ingenious backrest that allowed him to sit partially erect. Overhead was a latticed brush roof or sunshade, held up by forked corner poles that could also support similar side panels for full enclosure. Only one was presently in place, behind him, the others had been leaned against some nearby chaparral to afford unrestricted view from the primitive shelter.

Stanton's eyes characteristically sought the horizon first, probing the tremendous vista that separated his vantage from the far distance. It was the same on all three visible sides, a full two hundred and seventy degrees of limitless vision. He had seen much in this country that impressed him, but nothing to equal this. A man could step through the Pearly Gates themselves into this and not be disappointed.

The thought brought wry amusement. There

was a vague, curious feeling of familiarity, as though he had seen it before. This vast dapple of shadow and color and space. This lie and lift of land. This contour of country, unmarked and unclaimed. This strange feeling of peace and content. This sense of home.

He let his eyes travel slowly inward from the horizon to its center, where he lay. He saw that one of the voices belonged to the young Ute with whom he had ridden away from the wagon train. The other belonged to a girl. A young woman, actually. As wild and beautiful as the country.

She was long-legged, with a straight, proud back and good shoulders that carried firm, well-rounded breasts high. Her thick, gleaming jet hair fell in a heavy double-braid below her waist. Her creamy skin carried a faint undertone of the red earth underfoot.

Stanton knew at once that it was she with whom he had dreamed of sleeping. And he knew that he would survive. A man at death's door would not be so successful in transmuting fantasy into reality.

There was evidence of a stay of some days about the shelter. Wood was in supply and there was considerable ash under the fire. A small, bailed iron pot simmered over it. The remnants of a carcass of fresh meat hung from a corner-pole. He could hear the rill of a small stream nearby.

He wondered where the encampment of the

horse thieves was and was curious that this girl should have been left here alone with the boy. She leaned close again, her breasts thrusting into view in the sag of her dress top. She saw the shift of his eyes.

'*Graciadios!*' she murmured. 'He's awake.' And to Stanton, '*Cómo está, señor?*'

'*Vivo,*' he answered wryly. 'I live—*creo que sí.*'

She smiled and went to the fire for the pot. She returned, knelt beside him, and began to feed him with a pewter spoon while the boy watched anxiously from the other side. The broth was heavy, pungent, and medicinal, but Stanton relished it.

'Chato saw them shoot you,' the girl said. 'Tell him,' she ordered the boy.

The young Ute obeyed. Hagen had fired the shot. The description made that clear. It came as no surprise. Stanton remembered the earlier shot from behind, ostensibly at the fleeing Utes, which had missed and been passed off as accidental carelessness in the excitement of skirmish. Hagen had wanted another opportunity and had made it. He had freed their young hostage and sided with Stanton's proposal to attempt a trade wholly in order to set up his target again. And this time he had not missed.

Hagen. Hagen and Brock. And Bennett Royer. Royer had known. Some understanding had passed between Hagen and himself. And he would have cut himself in. A complete freight rig and cargo of trade goods to be disposed of and parceled up in Santa Fe. The cattle, too. All conveniently chargeable to the Utes, as far as others in the train knew. So it would have seemed to them. So they would swear if occasion demanded.

'Did they get the horses?'

The boy shook his head. When Stanton fell, Chato's uncle, head of the raiding party, feared for his nephew. The Indians charged the two remaining wagon men, forcing them into hasty retreat to save their own skins.

Later, when it was discovered the fallen man was somehow still alive, the Utes retrieved Stanton's weapons and horse, loaded him across it, and took him with them. They could do no less, Chato explained. This bleeding *yanqui* had saved his life with a drawn pistol when he had been captured.

Soon, however, it had become evident the wounded man could not survive further travel. The Utes had built this shelter and killed an antelope for food. With a practical notion of individual responsibility, Chato's uncle had ordered him to stay with his benefactor. The rest had continued on with the stolen horses.

'I did a bad thing after what you did for me,' Chato concluded uncomfortably. 'I was sure you would die soon and I did not like being left behind, so I followed them in a little while. I took your horse and guns because I did not

24

think you would need them any more.'

'He took this, too,' the girl added.

She reached into a buckskin shoulder-bag, not unlike the reticules of her eastern sisters, and brought out a blood-stained moneybelt, which Stanton had not yet missed from about his waist. He started to fumble with the lacing of one of its pockets.

'It's all there,' the girl assured him. 'A lot of gold for one man.'

He thought that if she could have seen the fields and pastures and stock and the proud white portico of Stanton Hall, she would believe the belt held little enough salvage.

'I did not get far before I met 'Mana,' Chato said. 'She made me bring everything back here to you.'

'Your sister?'

Chato seemed surprised. He glanced at the girl before answering, 'No. A friend.'

The girl urged more broth on Stanton. He sipped mechanically.

'Actually, I visit Chato's *rancheria* often, as they visit mine. I was there when his uncle and the horse raiders came in. They told me what happened out here. I did not care about you. I do not worry about *yanqui*. It is not their country. It is ours. But I thought Chato's uncle was wrong. I didn't think he should be out here alone with you. He is young and he does not yet know much about medicine for wounds.'

She paused and put her hand to Stanton's

25

face to feel for heat. It was the same touch he remembered from his dreaming. She seemed reassured.

'When I first saw you, I thought you would die soon, too. You must forgive Chato for that. He stayed with me. Now I think it is all right. I think he can go. His family will be worried about him. I will stay.'

Stanton nodded. The thought was agreeable. Chato asked for his name.

'Spencer Stanton.'

'Stanton'—Chato repeated carefully, rounding and softening the vowels in Spanish style—'I will remember. You will remember that I am Chato?'

There was a fierce young pride in the question, as though the name was already of importance in his world.

'I'll remember, Chato. *Gracias*.'

Without further farewell, the young Ute led his horse from behind the shelter, vaulted up, and rode westward toward the rise of the mountains and the midsummer snow on their peaks. The girl returned to the fire, and Stanton's eyes strayed out over the basin again. The land changed constantly in configuration and detail and scope as the light changed. The uncanny feeling of familiarity, of homeland, persisted. Stanton felt his will to live, bullet-battered to a faint ebb, beginning to surge again.

The girl came back and sank near him.

Together they watched the silhouette of Chato shrink ever smaller against the bulk of the westerly mountains.

''Mana,' he asked thoughtfully, 'who owns this land?'

She did not take her eyes from the lengthening shadows.

'We have a saying,' she answered. 'No one owns this land. The land owns us.'

Stanton was aware of a complex, instinctive, even primordial relationship, which he sensed but could not define.

'Yes. You'd have that feeling. All of you for all of it. But I didn't mean the whole country. Only this piece of it. This basin. Who owns that out there? Who holds title? Do you know?'

The girl looked out at the immensity before them. Her features softened, as a lover's might.

'They call it the Corona. Since Spanish times. A grant from the king to an old family. Long ago.'

'All that for one man—one family?' She nodded. 'Who owns it now?'

'A Mexican woman,' she said. 'The last of the family. You must rest now.'

She lowered the backrest, stretching him on his back, and tugged over two of the latticed brush sidewall screens, placing them so that Stanton's view was largely cut off. He closed his eyes momentarily to marshal his thoughts and almost immediately fell asleep. When he awakened, it was at her insistence. It was time for him to eat again.

As the twilight darkened, the great, empty basin shrank slowly to the scope of the firelight before the shelter. A chill flowed down from the mountains, scented with juniper and pine. Stanton slept again and dreamed that the girl slept with him.

At breakfast he discovered he could sit up more comfortably. His wound was high on the right side, safely wide of the spine and straight through, back to front, between ribs. It missed the lung in passage, for there was no tint of blood in his spittle and no internal difficulty with breathing. Both exit and entry had drained cleanly and were closing under 'Mana's bandaging. He was weak from shock and loss of blood, but the greatest damage seemed to be to muscle walls, aggravated by the short range and the size of the huge slug that had hit him.

'Mana brought him his rifle and powder belt and asked him to recharge the weapon for her. He would need meat now, a lot of it, and their supply was low.

'You had better watch how,' he suggested.

'I know how. It is just that I do not know such a fine gun.'

'You'll have a long ride back for another recharge if you miss your first shot.'

'If I get a shot, I won't miss.'

He laughed at her assurance.

'How long do you think your people will let

28

you stay here with me?'

'Until I think you are well enough to travel.'

'Be days yet. Just the two of us now. Won't they have some feeling about that?'

'Why?'

He was tempted to tell her about his dream and that it had recurred last night, but in his present condition it would be a wasted opportunity, too precious to squander. There would be a better time.

'No one will worry,' 'Mana assured him.

Stanton suddenly stiffened at a sound grown painfully familiar in recent weeks—the distant, lowing gut-call of an unbred heifer. 'Mana saw his curiosity. She slid a side-screen clear. On the heavily grassed slope of a shoulder half a mile away, beef were grazing, all heads in one direction. They already seemed too sleek to be what Stanton hoped.

'I rode after the wagons for awhile the first day to be sure they didn't send anyone else back after you,' the girl said. 'The cattle were following but already a long way behind. No one was with them. The wagon men paid them no attention. They had not been watered and some were dying. Several carcasses lay along the way they had come. But when the wind came up, they smelled the water here and turned toward the mountains. The wagon men did nothing. They just kept on. I don't understand.'

'The cattle are mine,' Stanton said. 'They

slowed the wagons. The freighters didn't think I'd put up enough money to cover that. They thought the beef would have no value in Santa Fe.'

'They're right. We have cattle. But mostly for hides.' She paused, her eyes dancing. 'I don't think you know much about cattle, *Señor* Spencer Stanton. I counted eighty-two that live. But they are all cows, so there will not be more.'

'I had four young bulls, but I lost them on the trail.'

'Naturally,' she said. She took the recharged rifle from him. 'They carry too much between their legs to go such a long way. The female can always last longer. Sleep now. Then eat again. The broth is just as good cold. It should last until I get back. With luck, it won't be long.'

She stepped out of the shelter and disappeared from his angle of view. When she reappeared she was on a tough little mountain pony, the rifle across her thighs, riding gracefully at an easy run toward a green thread of timbered bottoms below the grazing cattle—so much like a man and so much a woman.

An hour later he heard the faint, faraway crack of the Henry rifle.

*       *       *

On the seventeenth day, by the best count he

could make, Stanton awoke from his usual midday mending *siesta* to discover that he was again alone in the camp. But this time not only 'Mana and her pony were gone. So were the little iron saddle-kettle and the shoulder-bag that contained her other possessions.

His own horse had been caught up, saddled, and tied on the shady side of the shelter. His pistol, rifle, and powder belt were beside him. His heavy moneybelt was strapped awkwardly to his body beneath his shirt. A skewer of meat, browned for eating, smoked slightly over the ebbing fire. The rest of the venison carcass 'Mana had brought down with his rifle was gone.

He shoved into his boots, walked into the clear, and surveyed the horizon. The cattle had moved down into the bottoms for noon water, but no other living thing was visible. The girl had vanished.

They had talked of what he must do when the time came. To the south, beyond the malpais that marked the boundary of the basin in that direction, was the Rancho Mora, direct on the old Indian trade trail to Santa Fe. 'Mana had warned him that, as elsewhere in New Mexico in these times, a *yanqui* could not expect a warm welcome at Mora, but his Spanish would help. He could at least expect civility, and supplies would be available.

Mora was very old and much of its well-watered bottoms had been farmed since the times of the *anasazi*, the ancient ones who had built stone cities before there were horses. It maintained a commissary for the convenience of neighbors in the higher valleys of the Sangre de Cristos. Stanton could re-outfit himself there before heading on to Santa Fe in search of his commandeered wagon and freight and those who had taken them. But the cattle must remain here, at least for the time being. It would be weeks before they could travel further.

All this had been agreed, but Stanton had not realized he would face it alone. He had thought 'Mana would ride with him at least a part of the way, and he felt cheated of farewell and promise of return.

He went back into the shelter, picked up his belongings, and carried them to his readied horse. After scuffing out the embers of the fire, he wrapped the cooked piece of meat in his kerchief and tied it to a saddle-thong. He pulled easily up with his left hand, winced a little at the first movement of the horse, and found an easier position, favoring his wounded side.

It was a leave-taking as simple as from a casual midday stop on any trail he had ever ridden, yet he had spent seventeen days here in the company of a woman. When he looked back the smoke of the fire was gone from the sky and the shelter had merged into the upland chaparral on the banks of the little creek by which it stood.

Half an hour later, as 'Mana had promised, he struck a game trail and the old Indian road to Santa Fe.

## CHAPTER THREE

Felipe Peralta was seventy years old, all of which he had lived in the cottonwood-shaded *hacienda* of Rancho Mora. He was having a pre-supper *chocolate* in the cool of the *ramada* across the front of the old house when Abelardo came to him, hat in hand. Abelardo was young and fierce and the third of that name and family to be *segundo* of the rancho in Don Felipe's time.

'A *yanqui* comes,' the foreman reported. 'Through the malpais. From the Cimarron, I think.'

'Alone?'

Abelardo nodded.

'Bring him in.'

Abelardo showed a quick flash of disapproval.

'He has been hurt recently, *Patrón*. Shot, I believe. If he found enemies up there, he is our enemy, too.'

'Bring him in, 'Lardo,' Don Felipe repeated.

'Here?'

'No. The house is for guests. The store. I will

33

meet you there.'

Abelardo bent a little in deference and withdrew. Don Felipe knew his *segundo* preferred dealing with strangers in his own way. But he was the *patrón*. Such decisions were his. He regretted leaving his *chocolate* unfinished, but he stepped out into the ebbing heat of the dying day.

Some said the *yanquis* were a benefit. With those who came first only to trap the high country, Don Felipe thought this might be true. They were few. Their furs passed into Mexican hands at Taos or Sante Fe. They squandered what their trapline earned on *aguardiente* and women before they disappeared into the mountains again. They left their profits behind and no mark upon the country.

But these later ones were a different matter. They made a highway across the eastern desert. A highway for wagons. An incredible thing the Spanish and the Mexicans had not been able to accomplish in two hundred years. Don Felipe feared it. It was true the way was shorter than the ancient pack-trail along the *Camino Real* through Chihuahua to Mexico City. It was true that the goods they brought for sale were of better quality and greater variety and the prices far more reasonable than those from the homeland. But these new ones were businessmen and opportunists.

Felipe Peralta and others of wisdom feared

that these *yanquis* saw more of value in this distant province than the keepers of the Republic did. In Don Felipe's lifetime the *yanquis* had crossed the rivers and mountains of their own country and continued onto the waterless plains of the *llanos estacados* to claim half the continent. However much they talked of trade and mutual benefit, the real fear was that in the end it was land they were after. If they began to take up land, the old ways would be destroyed forever.

The stranger was already there when Don Felipe came into the public yard before the store. Abelardo was with him and the *segundo* had been right. The man had suffered recent severe injury. Almost surely a gunshot. He had dismounted and was seated on the tongue of a *carreta* to avoid the discomfort of standing. He came painfully to his feet at Don Felipe's approach.

'*Buenos días, señor.* You are the *hacendado*—you are Don Felipe Peralta?'

It was a Spanish Don Felipe had not heard since the time of his own grandfather. The language of the *conquistadores*, before the Castilian lisp had been lost to intruding Indian tongues. It was a rare accomplishment for a foreigner, but before he could ask about it Abelardo cut in harshly, snapping at the *yanqui*.

'One does not stand before the *patrón* with the head covered!'

'My friend,' the tall man answered wearily but without rancor, 'I don't take my hat off before God Almighty unless I am in His house.'

Don Felipe waved his *segundo* to silence. 'You speak the Spanish of a gentleman. Where did you learn it?'

'From a friend, *señor*. A man who once served me as this one does you. A Carib Indian who escaped to my country from the Spanish islands.'

'A Carib?' Don Felipe was genuinely surprised. 'From Hispaniola? I had supposed them all long dead. Who sent you here?'

'A band of Utes who befriended me. One of them, really. A girl. A young woman. They called her 'Mana.'

At mention of the name Don Felipe was instantly on guard. If this one had been told no more than that, there was a reason. He merely nodded and listened quietly to the man's account of an attack on a *yanqui* wagon train, a subsequent attack on himself, and his rescue. It seemed straightforward enough, in keeping with Ute raiding tactics and Don Felipe's private notion of *yanqui* perfidy, even to their own kind. But if the girl 'Mana had been as wary as was apparent, this *yanqui* would get no different treatment at Rancho Mora.

'A most unfortunate experience,' he said. 'I sympathize with your loss, but I must warn you. Santa Fe is changing. A foreigner can

36

expect little help from the law there these days.'

'I don't want help. I don't need it. I want to buy some gear to replace what I lost. That's all. It was cold last night without a blanket.'

Don Felipe shrugged.

'Of course. Allow *Señor* Stanton to purchase what he requires, 'Lardo. See that he has supper. There is clean fodder in the stable. He can sleep there.'

He turned away. The *yanqui* stopped him.

'Tell me about that girl up there.'

Felipe phrased his answer carefully, honestly with a minimum of information.

'There is not much. The home place of her people can't be far from where she found you. A small canyon north of the Cimarron, I believe. They say she went for a time to the mission school at Taos. Later to the convent at Santa Fe as well, I think. You were fortunate. The Utes are not always so friendly.'

'Do you see her?'

'Sometimes she comes to trade.'

'Good. The next time she does, will you tell her how grateful I am? She didn't give me the chance.'

The *yanqui* took gold American coins from his pocket in generous amount and offered them. Don Felipe refused with a curt shake of his head.

'The thanks, yes. Of course. The money, no. She would not accept. This is New Mexico, *señor.*'

The *yanqui* returned the gold to his pocket and followed Abelardo into the ranch store. Don Felipe did not go back to his *chocolate* as he had intended. He sat on the tongue of the *carreta* and waited. In a few minutes Spencer Stanton reappeared. He spread down his new blanket and wrapped his other purchases within, making a small, tight saddle-roll. He looked up as he worked.

'Beautiful country up there on the other side of the lava,' he said. ' 'Mana told me it's an old grant—the Corona, she called it. She seemed to think it's owned by a Mexican woman.'

Now Felipe Peralta understood the girl's wariness. And he was not misled by the casual questioning.

'At one time, I understand,' he agreed carefully.

'Someone who lives up in here some place?'

'One is not sure about such things these days. Times are changing. So are titles. The government makes new regulations. Sometimes there have been forfeitures. The governor has much power in these matters. The records are in Santa Fe. It is best to make inquiry there.'

For all its evasiveness, Don Felipe realized it was plainly a refusal to part with information, but the *yanqui* only smiled.

'I'll do that,' he said. 'When I have time. *Mil gracias.*' He carried his saddle-roll to his horse, tying it in place across the cantle. 'I'll not

38

trouble you for supper or a bedding place. I've lost too many days, already. *Adiós.*

'*Vaya con Dios*—'

Don Felipe's response was automatic. The man swung up and rode out of the yard. Abelardo came out of the commissary to watch his departure.

'A strange one,' Abelardo said with grudging respect. 'I'm glad that's all he wanted. It's good to see him go.'

Don Felipe rose stiffly. Advancing age brought wisdom and many certainties. A man faced them as he could.

'What he bought is not all he wants,' he said quietly. 'He goes, but he will be back. Have him followed until dark, 'Lardo. He may have changed his mind while he was here. See that he doesn't swing around to the north again. If he does, we must send 'Mana a message ahead of him. And send another *vaquero* around to the house. I think I must write a letter to the governor. It must go tonight.'

Abelardo nodded and hurried off. Don Felipe moved back toward the *hacienda*, thinking that his *chocolate* would be cold now and would have lost its flavor.

\*        \*        \*

For all its age and the vast area it administered, the capital of *Nuevo Méjico* was not large. It consisted of a dun huddle of stout adobe

39

houses, all of one floor and flat-roofed. They flanked narrow, twisting streets that followed the course of three arroyos down from the mountain above. The streets converged on a relatively small, level bench, high above the blue void of the Rio Grande canyon, far to the west. The plaza, the business establishments, and the heart of the City of the Holy Faith were in this flat area.

Stanton attracted little attention as he rode in. The people of Santa Fe seemed less hostile to Americans than Felipe Peralta had led him to believe. He felt relief. Hagen and Brock, wherever they were now, would be confident they had done their work well, out there on the Ute grass. Royer would be equally at ease. But if any of them were still in Santa Fe, a description of a suspect arrival, even a casual mention, would alert them at once. He could only hope for confrontation on reasonably equal terms when the time came, and he did not want to needlessly forego the advantage of surprise.

A small, tidy livery, a block or two from the plaza, attracted him and he left his horse there. He asked about rooms and was directed to an inn called La Fonda on the southeast corner of the central square.

He approached the inn by back streets. It proved to be a big, busy sprawl of a place about a large, walled and gated stock and wagon yard. Stanton thought it must be much like the ancient caravansaries of Asia, quite possibly patterned after them. Inquiry of a passerby revealed it was the official terminus of both the Santa Fe Trail and the long pack-road up through Chihuahua from Mexico City. As such, it was dangerously too public for his purposes. He wanted to ask about the freight string Bennett Royer had captained, but refrained.

Returning to the livery by the way he had come, Stanton found that a hostler's quarters at the rear were unoccupied and available. There was a cistern in back, which he was assured contained good water. He rustled a feed bucket and washed his body, bathing the rapidly healing wounds—a luxury he had been forced to forego since 'Mana left him.

He slept a little, but the dream of the girl beside him on the blanket did not recur, as it had not since he left the Ute shelter. When he awakened it was dark. He dressed, changing to a fresh, coarse, hand-woven Mexican cotton shirt that had been one of his purchases at Rancho Mora. The rest of his outfit was somewhat the worse for wear but would have to do until he recovered his possessions. Holstering his Navy Colt well back under the skirt of his jacket, he returned to the street.

Santa Fe was softer and kinder without the harsh light of day. Traffic had thinned. Music came from no definable place. The air was cool and pleasant after the heat. Those who had

41

labored during the day were astir now, enjoying the evening hour. There was much spotless white cotton. Sombreros were discarded. There was laughter and good nature. And to Stanton's surprise there was quite a number of women and girls, in two's and three's if unescorted, strolling with much less restraint and self-consciousness than he would have expected in a Spanish land. Some were openly, amusedly coquettish without seeming to incur disfavor among their elders. A feeling of easy and open friendliness was strong. Stanton warmed to it.

There was a small, candle-lit *cocina* across the way from the livery. Hungry, Stanton entered. He was offered a seat at the long common table and was presently served a plate of *carne asada*, swimming in stewed peppers. He wryly thought of 'Mana's statement that New Mexican cattle were raised for hides instead of beef. The meat chewed as though the leather went all the way through. But the meal was otherwise delicious and he relished it.

He was without silver and there was a stir when he tried to pay with his smallest gold coin. They did not have sufficient change at this early hour. Perhaps he could drop back later. Or *mañana*. Or any other time of his convenience. Nor would they accept the coin until proper change was available. He was wished good fortune and a pleasant evening. Despite the discomfort of his wounds and his missing wagon and cargo, he thought that he had chosen well when he chose this land.

Outside again he was drawn along by the current of strollers and presently entered the plaza. It was quite large for so small a city, perhaps two or three acres in extent. The treeless, ungrassed expanse of clean, hard-packed earth was surrounded by business houses, a corner of La Fonda, what appeared to be two or three residences of importance, a squat, bell-mounted adobe church, and the Palace of the Governors.

The *Palacio de los Gobernadores* occupied the entire north side of the plaza. It was a solid, thick-walled building, already more than two centuries old. He thought it had probably originally been a fortress as well as official residence and seat of government. A broad, covered porch extended for several hundred feet along the plaza, and there was indication of an extensive open patio within the hollow square of the massive building. This kind of porch, Stanton thought, more than any other structure, accounted for the pervasive feeling of solidity and permanence about the city.

Loungers were gathered in considerable numbers under the long porch, and he avoided it, turning instead along a shorter side of the plaza where there were several small shops advertising goods of both Mexican and Yankee manufacture. Most were open to evening trade, but one, under the sign of

43

'*Wetzel y Cia.,*' was closing as Stanton approached. Lights were already out within, and a small, shabbily dressed man with a thin, sharp face and an upright shock of prematurely whitened hair was pulling the street door closed to lock it behind himself.

As the shopkeeper bent over the lock, his back to the square, Stanton saw two men approaching in opposing traffic. One was Mexican, the other Yankee. The Mexican wore a handsome uniform and carried himself with the universally unmistakable arrogance of the professional military. The Yankee was equally well dressed in an outfit Stanton suddenly realized had come from his personal trunk in his missing wagon.

He otherwise would not have recognized Bennett Royer in time to avoid full-on meeting in the disadvantage of this crowd. The wagonmaster had evidently found a good barber since his arrival. His blistered face had been treated and healed sufficiently for a clean shave and hair trim. Together with his appropriated clothes, the effect was a complete transformation and quite striking, as glances from women strollers attested.

Swiftly sliding his gun from its holster and shielding it with his body, Stanton stepped from behind against the shopkeeper, prodding with the weapon. The little man needed no other order. He stiffened, straightened, and silently reopened the shop door. Stanton

44

pressed close after him and eased the door shut behind them. He let the shopkeeper turn, but kept him covered. They watched as Royer and his Mexican companion passed the darkened door panel. Neither man outside glanced within. Stanton slipped his gun back into its holster.

'Sorry, *señor*,' he said swiftly. 'I couldn't let them see me. I'll be back later to explain and apologize.'

He started to reopen the door. The shopkeeper stopped him.

'No need to follow now, *amigo*,' the little man said. Stanton was intrigued by the curious accent with which he spoke Spanish. 'They're easy enough to find, whenever you want them. You're a stranger. They know you?'

'The *yanqui* does.'

'*Señor* Royer. Yes. I have spoken with him. He was *capitan* of a string of freight wagons that arrived here two weeks ago from the States. They suffered an Indian attack and a wagon owner was killed. *Señor* Royer is attempting to dispose of his assets for the benefit of his estate. You have some interest in that affair?'

'I'm the man he thinks his men killed.'

The little man peered sharply at Stanton in the darkness.

'Come.'

He led the way through racks and tables of merchandise to a side door. Stanton followed

45

him through. The shopkeeper carefully closed the door. A match exploded and he lighted a kind of hurricane lamp. Stanton found himself in a small room containing a rough work table, on which the lamp stood, a chair, and a lumpy, blanket-covered cot—obviously the shopkeeper's living quarters. The little man peered at him again in the light of the lamp and chuckled.

'It was the Spanish that fooled me,' he said in an English tinged with the same accent Stanton had detected in his Spanish. 'A useful accomplishment on dark nights in this country. You heard what I do to the language. I'm Sol Wetzel. This is my store. And you're Spencer Stanton. You're a lucky man.'

Wetzel brought a bottle and two tin cups from under the cot and poured generously.

'Taos Lightning,' he continued. 'They tell me it's good whiskey. I wouldn't know. But it does its job. I've heard Royer's story. They all swore to it. Let's hear yours.'

Stanton hesitated, but he liked the bright, hard, deceptively youthful face, the ready sense of humor, and the quick, intelligent eyes. He repeated what he had told Felipe Peralta except, for brevity, the details of his rescue by the Utes and his convalescence.

'I'm not a brave man, Stanton,' Wetzel said as he refilled the cups. 'But I am a businessman, which means I am a gambler. Some gamble here, too! So I know when a man lies and when he tells the truth. You could say it's my stock in trade and not be too far wrong. As a consequence, I live and make a profit when the odds are against both. They think here that it's because I'm a Jew. I should tell them different.'

He leaned forward in sudden earnestness.

'I tell you because I want you to know. Maybe we can do some business. But I don't help you. I help myself. Understand?'

'Fair enough.'

'All right. Your cattle were abandoned when they thought you had been killed. Everyone in the train voted for that. They had lost enough time and there's no trade in beef here.'

'So I've been told.'

'So?' Wetzel asked. 'Well, just in case you hadn't. Your wagon and teams were sold as salvage to one of the freighters. He took the rig back up the Trail when the train started back to the States, five or six days ago. They don't waste much turn-around time.'

'Salvage, hell! That was my property.'

'I know. But it was a legal sale, under the laws here. You will do something about it, I suppose. Maybe you can make Royer and those who stayed behind with him account to you. Figure twice what you paid for it and you'll just about have the going price in Santa Fe.'

'I'll get a damned sight more than that out of those bastards!'

'So they owe you, so all right again,' Wetzel

said impatiently. 'I told you I'm not a brave man. I don't make words. I make deals. What's an eye for an eye and a tooth for a tooth unless the eye is diamond and the tooth gold? When you get something, get money, man! Money—property—profit. Not satisfaction. Wait. Until the time is right. Tonight your wagon and teams are gone. Nothing can be done about them for now. But something can be done about the trade goods you were bringing to Santa Fe.'

'They haven't been sold?'

'No. But Royer thinks they have. To me. On authority of an order signed by the governor. They were delivered to my back room before the train left. That's why I didn't want them to see me, either, out there a few minutes ago. Royer's pressing me for payment.'

'You can't pay him for my goods.'

'It's simpler than that. I can't pay anybody. Months ago I ordered as much new inventory as I could afford. My order came in on the train you were with. I have little capital and a Jew never makes as much profit as his neighbors imagine. It took all my cash for the order and freight. I can't raise a sou more.'

'Then why even talk a deal with Royer?'

'Because this is Santa Fe. You saw him out there with Lieutenant Montoya. They have become friends. Easy to arrange with a few Yankee dollars. The lieutenant is prefect of the governor's guards. He has influence at the *palacio.* The governor wishes to encourage foreign investment here. He can be quite insistent. He doesn't want profit to leave New Mexico.'

Wetzel grimaced irritably.

'They think I have a fortune buried somewhere. It was suggested that I buy your goods. So Royer and his partners can be persuaded to reinvest in something else of benefit to the province, of course. Suggested, mind you. Not ordered. But here it is the same thing.'

'Now wait a minute!' Stanton protested incredulously.

'I know,' Wetzel said with a weary shake of his head, *'mishugenah.* But no crazier than what you've told me, right? Take the word of an honest man. They have me by the short hair. Business permits can be revoked. New taxes levied. Customers intimidated. But not if those goods were stolen from my storeroom, eh? What could they do? It's my only way out. And I can tell you how to sell your shipment at a greater profit than you'd ever get here. Do we talk business?'

Unbidden, Stanton sloshed more of the strong, clear, colorless local whiskey into his cup.

'I'm listening.'

'Where are you putting up?'

Stanton described the little livery. Wetzel nodded thoughtfully.

49

'I planned tomorrow night, but I've stalled too long already. Tonight's better. I was going to hire it, but the risk is too great that way. For me. And you should share it. If you fail, you may still have some kind of legal right. Even before the governor. I wouldn't. But you'll have to stay out of sight—'

The trader paused and looked keenly at Stanton. He seemed to reach a reluctant decision.

'All right. You trust me; I trust you. You'll stay here.'

He dragged the cot aside and scuffed in the dirt floor beneath it, revealing a heavily planked little trapdoor. He heaved it up, exposing a ladder descending into a black hole.

'If someone came looking for me and forced the door—and it has happened before—it wouldn't do for them to find you. I'll get your horse and gear and make arrangements. I won't be any longer than I have to. There's water in the cistern. Take this for light.'

He thrust the lamp into Stanton's hand. Stanton stepped onto the ladder.

'You'll find out a lot about Sol Wetzel down there,' the trader said. 'Get some sleep. You'll need it.'

As Stanton's head descended below the level of the floor, the trap closed above him.

# CHAPTER FOUR

The cellar in which Stanton found himself seemed to underlie a good portion of the store above. Shelving was stacked with all manner of treasure. There were strings of brilliantly colored Mexican peppers, sun-cured in the dry air. There were bales of fleshed and tanned hides and furs, some of them the finest he had ever seen. There were stacks of hand-woven Indian blankets and rows of highly glazed native potteryware, some of which he realized must be very old. There were several casks of wine and numerous smaller kegs he thought might contain eastern whiskey. There was a large, open crate of native uncut turquoise and matrix and boxes of other desert stones of unknown worth.

The mingling smells in the dead air were exotic and indefinable. Stanton realized that if Sol Wetzel did not have buried gold, this hidden storehouse alone made him a rich man. He began to feel that he had made a valuable ally. Stretching out on a stack of Indian blankets, he blew out the lamp and resigned himself to await the trader's return.

He thought it was after midnight when he roused to footfalls above and relit the lamp. The trap was lifted and Wetzel descended with the bottle of Taos Lightning and the cups.

Stanton declined. Wetzel filled his to brimful.

'I need it,' the trader said. 'My father taught me to buy and sell and trade to advantage, but I am not cut out for any other kind of thief. It settles in my stomach. Tonight of all nights. Nobody sleeps in Santa Fe. I swear it.'

'Do you think Royer suspects anything?'

'From a dead man? No. But that isn't all of the risk. The governor would not approve of this, you know. It will be quite an embarrassment to him. Thieves right across the plaza from his *palacio.* A hard thing to explain if word ever got to Mexico City. He is very sensitive about such things.'

Wetzel sucked deeply from his cup, coughed, and continued.

'The guards were out later than usual. Three parties. One with Lieutenant Montoya and Royer. The other two with your friends Hagen and Brock. Maybe they were looking for me, but they would have come in if they were, I think, and the lock wasn't touched. But it's quieted down now. They've all gone back to the *palacio* for a few rounds of *aguardiente.*'

'You're sure?'

'On the best authority.' Wetzel turned and called up through the open trap. 'Jaime, come on down here.'

A slight figure descended the ladder. It was the boy whom Royer had bullied into involuntary servitude on the Trail.

'Jaime—a good name,' Wetzel said. 'Such

52

things are important. Names. Look at history. Jaime's the same in Yiddish and Spanish, except for the spelling, right? And both better than in English. You know each other.'

Stanton nodded. The boy remained silent and apprehensive.

'You'll forgive me,' Wetzel continued to Stanton. 'No doubt of you. Natural precaution. A habit I can't break. To hear the story of your quarrel with Royer from somebody else. Jaime obliged. He seems to have some regard for you. And he wants to get away from Royer. We'll give him the chance. No?'

'If he knows what he's getting into. Which is more than I do.'

'I know, all right, Mr. Stanton,' Jaime said. 'I—I'm sorry about what happened to you. None of the rest of us on the wagons knew anything about it. We thought it was the Indians. Honest.'

'It's all right, son.'

'And I thought I was being crowded!'

'Jaime has just come from the *palacio*,' Wetzel continued. 'He wanted to get his belongings from the rooms Lieutenant Montoya has given Royer there. They're gambling with some of the guards and didn't even notice him. Their bottles are full and they'll be at it until morning.

'Now, let me explain to both of you. Three days down the river on the *Camino Real* is the small town of Albuquerque, a young colony of many farms. Goods reach it only from Mexico City. Governor Pérez sees to it that Yankee goods are not shipped there. He wants to keep that advantage for Santa Fe. To the people he uses the excuse that the trail south is impassable to wagons, and to make sure it is he maintains his own guards and won't support federal troops here. General Armijo, a very ambitious man, has a lot of property near Albuquerque and doesn't care for this. But what can he do about it? He and his people have need of what you are carrying and will pay well for it. I've made up an inventory and what it should be worth to them.'

The trader handed Stanton a sealed list. Stanton started to break the seal. Wetzel stopped him.

'Later. No time now. Remember. Technically you're not only thieves but smugglers. But if you reach Armijo, you won't have to worry further about Royer and his partners or Montoya and his guards. Or even Governor Pérez. The governor and the general have a certain respect for each other.'

He picked up the lamp and climbed the ladder. Stanton and Jaime followed. Wetzel led the way out into the darkened public room of the store. Stanton saw through the front windows that the plaza had completely emptied of traffic. The only light showing was in a couple of the small, high windows on the far side of the *palacio.*

A door at the rear of the store let them into the storeroom. It, too, was unlighted. Shadowy figures were soundlessly carrying crates and boxes and kegs and bundles out into an alleyway.

A string of pack burrows waited in patient silence there. Stanton saw his saddled horse, rifle in place and his saddle-roll lashed to the cantle. The other horse he supposed was for Jaime. Most of the packs were already tarped and lashed. As Wetzel's men finished loading and closing the others, Stanton made a count of the string and turned accusingly to the trader.

'There's a hell of a lot more in those packs than my wagon carried.'

Wetzel seemed surprised at the accusation.

'But of course,' he agreed. 'If you're to get better prices in Albuquerque than can be had here, why not me, too? There's no profit in an overlooked opportunity, my friend. I've added a few packs. They're on the inventory. When you trade with the general, some of it will be on commission for me.'

Stanton dubiously eyed again the now completely laden string of pack animals.

'How many men do we get?'

'One,' Wetzel said complacently. 'To lead you the best way out of the city. Why more? If you're overtaken and discovered, it would be foolish to stand and fight. And I can't ask any others to take the risk. Some don't love the governor, but they're natives—his people. Their lives would be in real danger if they were with you and you're caught.'

Stanton saw that the silent, shadowy laborers were drifting away, vanishing into the night. Only one remained, beside the lead burrow. He nodded to Jaime and they mounted. He looked down at Wetzel.

'You son of a bitch,' he said, 'you'll be a millionaire before you're through.'

The trader smiled as though at deserved praise. 'Or a dead Jew,' he added.

Stanton rode toward the head of the string. The man waiting there led off on foot and the laden burros followed, each haltered to the pack ahead at two-pace intervals. Jaime, as though he knew exactly what was expected of him, lingered to bring up the rear. They moved out of the alleyway into one of the twisting, sleeping streets of Santa Fe, unshod hoofs making little sound in the dust of the unpaved way.

In a few minutes houses fell away and they reached the edge of the city at a broad ford of the bright, brisk little stream of the Rio de Santa Fe. Their guide left them here, indicating the dusty, deep-worn track of the *Camino Real* resuming on the southern bank. Here Jaime came up and began to free each animal's halter, looping the free end back onto its own pack. Stanton protested, afraid that giving the animals free head would make them more difficult to handle and keep from straying.

'They'll string along all right, Mr. Stanton,' the boy assured him. 'They like it best this way and they'll move along faster. Maybe gain as much as five miles a day. That's important, isn't it?'

'To me,' Stanton agreed. 'You seem to have a hand with them, all right. Where from?'

'Bred with them,' Jaime answered. 'Folks think we raise mules. Back in the Missouri hills, where I come from, this was all we had. Jacks and hogs. Hell, I never saw a horse till I was nine nor a wheel till I was twelve, excepting on a busted-down barrow by my grandpappy's outhouse. I get along with jacks and jennies real good. I wouldn't of come along if I didn't think I could be of some use.'

'Makes you welcome enough,' Stanton told him. 'Don't fret about it.'

Halters and pack girths to his satisfaction, Jaime remounted and rode alongside Stanton.

'You've got your pistol. I'd admire to have that rifle on my saddle, just in case.'

'In case what?' Stanton asked, amusing himself as much as anything else.

'In case they come after us,' the boy said soberly.

'Think they will?'

'Would if it was me. Don't see no reason for them to be no different.'

Stanton surrendered the rifle.

'Can you use it?'

'Took two squirrels to make a pie at our table. We didn't have no powder and shot to spare. Never had a supper cost me more'n one shot.'

Stanton smiled. 'You're getting more welcome by the minute. Take the lead for a while. Keep them to the center of the trail. Been so many strings over it nobody can tell whether we have or not.'

Jaime nodded. 'Till we pull off for water and grass.'

He rode ahead and the animals began to move again, each docilely following the one ahead, and Stanton saw their pace was quicker.

The *Camino Real* pulled gradually away from the Rio de Santa Fe, lining more or less due south for the Rio Grande at Albuquerque rather than following the smaller stream westerly to its confluence with the river. In about three hours they came to another small rill slanting down toward the valley floor. Stanton became aware of the dust in his mouth and rode forward to suggest a halt.

Jaime was strangely reluctant. Burros were easily good for a day without water. Too much in their bellies slowed them. Best to water and grass at the same time and there was no good graze nearby. They were underway and making good time. Why delay? The cool of the night was the most pleasant time to travel. Stanton realized at once that something was wrong and cut through the protestations, forcing the truth from the boy.

'Mr. Wetzel was right,' Jaime said uncomfortably. 'They'll be at their rotgut and cards in the *palacio* till morning. But Mr. Wetzel's going to have to raise a ruckus over being robbed if he's going to make it stick. And the minute he does, they're going to know who did it and why.'

'How?'

'Because they know you're not dead, that you're on your way to Santa Fe. Some rancher up north sent a message to the governor. Told him all about you. That's why Brock and Hagen and Royer haven't crowded Mr. Wetzel any more than they have. Waiting for you to show up. That's who they were looking for tonight. Each one of them with a bunch of guards to recognize you if you were spotted. They aimed to get you before you could talk to anybody. A wanted man trying to resist arrest, or something. The guards would make it look legal enough and with the wagon train gone, nobody else in town would realize who you really were.'

Quick, exasperated anger came up in Stanton.

'Oh, God! Why the hell didn't you tell us? Wetzel and I could have changed the plan. It wasn't all that good in the first place.'

'That's why,' Jaime said miserably. 'You'd have stayed in town. And they'd of got you, sure. A lot of people must have seen you before you got to Wetzel's. And they'd all know you're a stranger. They'd of heard about it at the palace, sooner or later, and they'd of found you. Even if they had to dig you out from under Mr. Wetzel's store.' Jaime paused, then added with painful honesty, 'And I'd have had to stay with them.'

'Well, it's done,' Stanton said resignedly. 'No matter what kind of a fancy lie poor Wetzel tries on them, it won't take any kind of genius for them to know who pulled his "robbery" and where we're headed. No stopping here, that's sure. We've got between fifty and sixty miles to go. Another hour till daylight. Two more for them to find out what's happened, and they'll be on our tail. We'll have to find us a hole, then, and try to pull it in after us. Come on. Let's move!'

They crossed the creek without permitting a burro to water. Stanton slipped a halter from one of the animals and ranged back and forth along the string, swinging the halter and trying to haze the string to a faster pace. A few of the burros broke into a short, jolting trot for a few paces, but no more. And the unhaltered one kept breaking from the line, straying from the dusty track to browse at the nearest tuft of bunch-grass. Stanton grew irritable at the straying tracks. At length Jaime loped back along the string.

'It won't work, Mr. Stanton,' he said

apologetically. 'A jack goes his own rate. There's slower, but no faster. He'll keep up with the rest. That's all. And slipping his halter means he's through work for the day.'

Stanton dismounted and replaced the borrowed halter. The wayward burro reluctantly nosed back to its place in the line. Jaime rode back to the head of the string and they went on. Stanton remained on foot, leading his horse, for a quarter of a mile or so. He found that Jaime was right. The plodding string maintained a surprisingly steady pace. He thought it would average a little better than three miles an hour. Perhaps a third better than the rate to which his stock had held the wagon train. But Albuquerque was still many such hours away.

Stanton remounted and began to ride ahead a couple of miles periodically to make certain they didn't come unexpectedly on the night camp of another string or a roadside habitation that might later report their passage. Fortunately he encountered none. He was relieved. If they had to quit the trail to circle such a hazard, they would leave a clear and fresh sign of their detour for an alert tracker.

Day began to come on. This was one dawn Stanton did not enjoy, as he watched the horizon begin to take shape behind them. He discovered himself searching for signs of pursuing horsemen when he knew it was far too soon for any to appear. Westward mountains beyond the Rio Grande, thirty or forty miles away, took first light. The red stone of their escarpments emerged purple from the night black, growing slowly more brilliant in the low-slanting rays of the rising sun.

The mountains to the east, towering directly above them, cast a great long shadow across the trail and far down into the valley of the Rio Grande. When the sun at length crested their peaks, lifting night chill, it was welcome. The burros plodded steadily on with Jaime riding in the lead like a kind of silent Pied Piper.

In about two hours the boy pulled up at a small creek that traced a thin line of green up a draw into the folding of the mountains and timber reaching down from above.

'We better be getting off the trail pretty soon now, Mr. Stanton,' he said with a worried frown. 'May be as good a place as we'll hit. Looks like three or four miles to any kind of cover up there, and a pretty stiff climb, too. But the creek's shallow enough to travel, and if we keep to the stream bed, we shouldn't leave any tracks to amount to anything.'

Stanton shook his head and pointed off in the opposite direction. Far down into the valley, its adobe walls and roof hard to separate from the colors of the land, a tiny house huddled on the creek bank. There was no smoke above it, but the hour was yet early, and an irrigated field was a green postage stamp beside it.

'We could probably keep out of line of sight on the way up, all right,' Stanton said. 'But if we stayed in the creek any distance, we'd be bound to really roil the water up. Drift would carry a long ways with this much fall. Dry as that country is down there, they'd watch their water. If anybody's down there, they'd know something was going on up here by the color. Take the hour and the closeness of the trail and it wouldn't be too hard to figure out.'

The boy nodded unhappily and took the burros on across the stream. Presently the shoulder they had been traveling leveled into a broad unmarked flat. There was no discernible cover more than fetlock high. Stanton measured the distance to more broken country on the far side in terms of time, and his jaw set. But they had no choice. The trail cut straight across and they didn't dare leave it. In such terrain their tracks would be an open invitation the moment they turned from the ancient way.

Heat began to build up uncomfortably and the burros' hides darkened with sweat beneath their packs. One or another began to bray occasionally in protest. The sound, Stanton realized, was as unmistakable as a cavalry bugle and would carry an enormous distance in the clear air of this silent land. At each outburst he instinctively looked behind. But there was no visible movement, no distant dust of passage.

A little past midmorning, when Stanton was sure they had used up all of the lead to which they were reasonably entitled, thunderheads began to build over the red mountains, across the river to the west. They tumbled up in prodigal splendor, dwarfing the mountains themselves, obscuring a quarter of the horizon. A strong downslope wind developed on the slopes of the closer mountains on the east and swept across the flats they were traversing, forming a giant churn above the whole valley of the Rio Grande. The burros ceased their braying and put their heads down as they plodded on.

Lightning began to flicker about the darker peaks of cloud. Muted thunder began to mutter ominously and the storm wall, multiplying itself incredibly as it moved, tumbled swiftly across the valley toward them. The wind stiffened and the heads of the burros dropped lower. Stanton realized rain was certain. And the pulverized dust of the *Camino Real*, which recorded nothing when dry, once wet, would indelibly record recent passage until the hoofs of subsequent pack trains could cut it to powder again.

It was Jaime who spotted the dust, far back up on the shoulder from which they had descended. It was caught by the wind and was a streamer of drift, so its immediate source could not be determined, but neither had any doubt it was the pursuit they anticipated. It was also obvious that in their exposed position in the middle of the flat, they were certain to become visible to those behind within a few minutes. And the storm could not reach them before then.

At this point the ground suddenly fell away before them into a narrow, shallow, young cutback or barranca, probably no more than two or three seasons old, cut by storm waters rather than natural drainage. It was dry, sand-floored, and sufficiently deep to keep their heads below the rim if they dismounted and led their horses. Stanton immediately turned the burros up its course.

Proof that it was a reasonably secure shelter lay in the fact that the cutbank itself had not been visible to them from above or indeed until they were practically upon it, but Jaime was concerned about the tracks they cut in the smooth, windblown sand of its floor as they turned from the pack trail. Stanton did not explain that he was counting on the building thunderstorm. That, in itself, was another hazard he did not want to meet until he was forced to.

After perhaps a mile and half a hundred twisting meanders of the cutbank, Stanton lagged back and climbed to the eye-level of the bank. Their pursuit was just coming down from the mountain shoulder onto the flat. At this reduced distance it was easy to separate the stiffer Yankee silhouettes of Royer, Hagen, and Brock from the instinctive superior horsemanship of the Mexican guards who rode with them. In all, a party of about twenty.

The stiffening wind blew sand from the grass roots into Stanton's eyes. And with it came the first sting of rain. Thunder crashed and the distant horsemen were erased by the sweeping sheets of the approaching storm. Stanton was soaked before he was back to his horse. The sandy floor of the arroyo began to darken as it sucked thirstily at the water. Stanton kicked up his horse and rode fast past the string and Jaime to scout ahead. He knew he might not have much time.

After the first few sheets of water, riding the wind, the rain came steadily, so torrentially that it hammered the earth with a rising roar that drowned out the sound of the wind. The air dropped degrees in moments to a chill that cut through soaked clothing. Pockets between the bunchgrasses of the flat filled quickly and began to run together. Little rivulets formed and spilled over the lip of the cutbank, trickling in tiny mud torrents down the walls, eroding the red earth away as they ran. The sand softened and grew wetter underfoot.

A quarter of a mile farther on, one of the meanders of the barranca had been cut through, making a little island less than an acre in extent. It had been washed over, grass and several layers of topsoil swept away at some previous time, so that it stood perhaps three or

66

four feet above the sandy floor and five or six feet below the level of the banks.

It was a dubious enough haven at best, but Stanton saw that the spill from the banks was already uniting in a turgid stream on the barranca floor and the rain seemed to be hammering down harder by the moment. He wheeled back toward the pack string.

The burros had slowed with the onslaught of the storm, but Jaime seemed to comprehend what might be coming. Keeping the animals moving, he was working feverishly back along the string, making each halter fast to the pack ahead again, so that the chain could not be broken. Stanton caught up the lead halter and dallied it about the horn of his saddle, putting a strain on that pulled up the lead burro's head and literally dragged it into a faster pace. Jaime urged the others on as he worked.

By the time they reached the island, the burros were splashing through knee-deep, red-brown water, running bank to bank down the barranca floor. They needed no urging to scramble up onto the higher ground of the island. There was no letup in the rain and no talking above its din, to which was now added the ominously deepening sound of the free-running, swiftly rising water on the barranca floor.

Jaime put their horses into a ring of burros and closed it by making the halter of the lead animal fast to the pack of the last. Stanton knew that if the current increased, or if the string parted and any of the animals slipped into the ugly stream, they would be capsized and drowned by the weight of their packs. He would have liked to unsaddle them and perhaps use the packs as a bulwark against the rising water, but he knew it would be a wasted effort. The packs were securely enough tarped to withstand the rain, but not inundation. And if the water got high enough, they would be carried away. So he had to be content to leave them in place. Jaime looked at the water, then at him, and shook his head. It was an eloquent expression of Stanton's own doubt.

Suddenly, with a terrific multiple roll of thunder, the storm passed over them as swiftly as it had arrived. The rain did not slacken but stopped completely, as instantly as it had started. But it was sweeping on toward higher ground and Stanton continued to watch anxiously the water eating greedily away at the soggy little island on which they stood.

After a few minutes he thought the level was beginning to fall a little. Then he became aware of a new sound, low in pitch but seeming to shake the ground. Jaime grabbed his arm and pointed. A wall of water was coming toward them, debris tumbling on its crest run-off from somewhere upstream. The crest was only three feet or so above the level of the stream churning past on both sides of them, but their island was already awash, its edges rapidly flaking away. They only had time to get some of the burros braced head-on to the current before it struck with astonishing force.

Stanton felt his feet being swept from beneath him and he caught at the nearest pack to keep from going down.

## CHAPTER FIVE

Bennett Royer had always believed he had a special instinct. A kind of intermittent sixth sense passed down by a similarly gifted individual in the tangled skein of unknown forebears. Others dismissed it, sometimes with envy, as simple hunch, but he had stronger convictions.

Too many times he knew beforehand which way a disputed situation would go and profited thereby. Too many times he knew when he could stand and when he could not, so saving his life and costing others theirs. It was the sole basis of the luck that usually attended his play at cards. When it came, it came clearly, without any muck of uncertainty.

Sitting on rising ground, to which they had retreated, where the trail came down onto the flats where the rain caught them, he watched the storm roll on up into the mountains, lightning flashing and thunder muttering distantly among the peaks. Hagen and Brock sat hunched on their mounts, their fire damped out by the rain. This wasn't their style. In any but fair weather, at least. Too much work and discomfort. The shot in the back, the quick knife, the pistol-slugging suited them best. The small stakes that were easiest to come by. These men were useful enough on occasion, as in that dry camp out on the Trail—even if they had muffed it—but not to be counted on in a big bind. Worthless bastards, with no real purpose beyond living from one day to the next. But no problem. Merely necessary evils, easy enough to dispose of when their usefulness was done.

He looked at Luis Montoya and his Mexican guards, sitting patiently in their wet saddles, untroubled by the sudden, slashing downpour that had swept the flat before them. This was their country. They were used to it. What got wet would dry. Beans, bread, a bottle, and a uniform to wear. Better than labor in the mud and sun.

Montoya was different. He had ambition, in his way. And his connection with Governor Pérez. But essentially he was as worthless a bastard as Paul Hagen. Just trickier. And so he had to be watched more closely.

Royer reined over to the lieutenant and extended his hand for his saddle glass. Montoya handed it to him and Royer put it to his eye, extending the tubes for focus. His instinct told him Spencer Stanton was out

70

there somewhere. The polished, arrogant, tough-fibered son of a bitch. And the kid who had turned traitor after all Royer had done for him on the Trail and after they'd gotten to Santa Fe.

Spencer Stanton and the kid. Not on the flat below them, maybe. There had been no sign of them before the storm. But not far beyond. A few miles at most. With the stake he was playing for loaded onto a string of pack-jacks. The stake he needed to ante into a bigger game. The goods Sol Wetzel reported stolen from his back room. Goods that belonged to Bennett Royer by any rule of the game, the way he played it. Wetzel. The goddamned lying little Jew!

The sun had broken through the after-clouds of the storm and a flash of reflection from water crossing the track of the *Camino Real*, about midway across the flat below, caught Royer's glass. He saw the reflection was from a flash stream, indicating there was a dry course there that had not been visible before. There was no way at this angle to detect the direction the run took or the width and depth of the channel it had cut. The flow was only revealed at the hoof-sloped banks where the trail forded it, but the sure knowledge came. He knew where Stanton and his pack string had taken shelter.

Royer collapsed Montoya's glass and handed it back to the lieutenant.

'Nothing,' he said. 'What do you think?'

'Old tracks washed out,' the Mexican answered. 'No way to miss new ones, once they start to move again, or even if the storm didn't stop them. We'll have them sure in a couple of hours.'

'No,' Royer said. 'Stanton's too smart. That rain made him hole up. He'll stay holed up till he's got dry ground to travel.'

'Then we'll have to find where. You heard the governor's order. Those goods aren't to get through to Albuquerque.'

'To General Armijo, you mean,' Royer corrected with a grin. 'That's another thing. We bear on much further south, we'll be getting into the general's territory. The governor was just as pointed about that. He doesn't want us tangling with Armijo's friends.'

Montoya signaled with his head and rode off a few yards to be out of earshot of his guards and the other two Yankees. Royer followed. The lieutenant was scowling.

'*Qué pasa, amigo?*' he asked in complaint. 'If we don't bring back the pack train, where is the profit? I have an interest in this matter, too'— Montoya checked himself suspiciously—'if you intend to keep your promise about that.'

'I'll keep it,' Royer said easily. 'Don't worry about that. But tell me this: if we take those packs back to Santa Fe, what will they bring?'

'Santa Fe prices. It's already been agreed. If

72

not *señor* Wetzel, then some other trader with enough money. I told you that the governor will see to that.'

'Sure. But suppose we have a little bad luck. Suppose we lose Stanton through no fault of ours. Supposing he gets through to Albuquerque and sells them to Armijo's people. What'll they bring then?'

Montoya began to smile.

'Such a misfortune could happen. The storm and all. And of course they will pay more in Albuquerque. Much more gold.'

'That's what Wetzel and Stanton figured, too. That's why Stanton decided to risk this instead of facing Brock and Hagen and me down in Santa Fe. What's good for him right now is good for us. Money's a hell of a lot easier to handle than a string of burros and some rain-soaked packs. When Stanton collects it, he's got to come back to Santa Fe. Right to us. There's no place else for him to go. Just how much general hell do you think the governor will raise if we go back empty-handed and let Stanton do our work for us?'

Montoya scrubbed his cheek slyly.

'He'll be much embarassed that General Armijo will have *yanqui* goods for his people in Albuquerque. He won't like that. There's no love lost between them, and Armijo runs Albuquerque as if it is a province of its own. Both complain to Mexico City about their disagreements. But Governor Pérez can be a reasonable man. If there is much profit and a sufficient tax for the government'—the lieutenant shrugged—'it can be arranged.'

Royer nodded and gigged his horse. They rode back to the others. Hagen scowled at them.

'What the hell's going on?' he complained peevishly.

'We've lost them. We're going back.'

'You lost your *cojones?*' Hagen protested. 'Without Stanton we got nothing. We get him or he gets us.'

'We'll get him. He can't get away. But there's easier ways than this.'

Hagen shrugged disinterestedly, without further comment. Brock straightened uncomfortably in his saddle.

'If you say so, it suits me,' he growled. 'I could do with a bottle and a double-breasted little bed-warmer about now.'

Montoya raised in his stirrups and signaled his men.

'*Vámonos! Se marcha!*'

Royer fell in with his two companions behind the governor's guards and they took the slope above them toward Santa Fe. He rode at ease, little troubled by wet clothing and the prospect of the long ride ahead. Let them call them hunches if they wanted. But they were better than that. A hell of a lot better. And if a man didn't play them, he was a fool. This was only the first hand and the game was already set up.

The capitol of *Nuevo Méjico* was hardly his town, but a hell of a hunk of it was sure going to be.

*         *         *

Three burros went down in the first swirling rush of the crest, threshing wildly against the unbalancing bouyancy of their tarped packs, but the haltered ring of animals held, others anchoring those swept from their feet. With Jaime's knowing help, Stanton got the downed ones up again almost immediately, and, he thought, with negligible water damage to the goods they carried. After the first surge of the passing crest in those few wildly struggling moments, the water began to drop almost as fast as it had risen.

The problem now was that the little island upon which they had taken refuge had turned into a quagmire underfoot. Stanton was concerned over the possibility of quicksand. However, as the water continued to drain, it revealed a slick, soapy, incredibly clinging bed of red adobe that made tough going but was passable.

As soon as the animals were straightened out and Jaime had them under control again, Stanton fought his way to the north bank of the little barranca and wormed up the clinging, slippery sidewall until he could drag himself out onto the grass of the now steaming flat.

Their pursuit was not where he had last seen it before it was screened off by the swiftly advancing rain front. He searched the intervening area anxiously, although he knew there was no concealment there for a single rider, let alone so large a party. Then his eyes lifted to the slope beyond, scarred by the visible track of the *Camino Real*, and he saw the riders. To his surprise they were retracing their own track, departing. He remained prone, watching them go out of sight, to be certain.

When he slid back to the floor of the cutbank, Jaime burst into laughter.

'You look like an old boar that's been rooting in a brickyard.'

Stanton grinned.

'You wouldn't take any prize in a pattern book yourself. They say sitting horseback makes a man out of a farmer. Let's see if it does anything for this mud. Better than wading in it, anyway.'

He started to remount. Jaime was alarmed.

'They'll see us, sure!'

Stanton pulled on to saddle.

'They're gone. Back where they came from.'

Jaime also stepped uncertainly to stirrup, standing to peer across the empty flat. Stanton pointed out to him the place where he had seen their pursuit disappear in retreat. Jaime scowled, troubled.

'Now, why'd they do that? Ben Royer'd have

a reason. A good one.'

'He got smart. One of them did. What they ought to have done in the first place. We've got to come back, sooner or later, too, you know.'

Jaime sobered even more. Stanton saw that this was something about which the boy had not thought.

'That's for another day, son,' he said reassuringly. 'We can't get up these banks. Won't be dry enough before tomorrow. Might as well go back down to the ford at the trail and do it the easy way. Then find a place to pull off and dry out. With nobody on our tail, we can afford to take it some easier than we have been.'

Jaime smiled with a rueful shake of his head.

'Jacks are going to like that news about as fine as I do.'

He started the string and the burros followed his horse, stepping down from what remained of their island onto the barranca floor, now again running scarcely more than fetlock deep.

Stanton, once more bringing up the rear of the muddy, splashing, plodding string, wondered in retrospect at the quick-changing, violent moods of this land. A summer shower was all it had been, less than an hour from first thunderhead to last roll of thunder, yet it had built up all the turbulence and power and proportionate deluge of a full-blown storm system. He realized the mistake he had made in trying to find shelter in the little dry barranca.

If the rain had lasted a little longer or had localized, the barranca would have become an inescapable death trap. He shrugged good-naturedly. A man learned his lesson or he died. That was the law. It was the same everywhere.

An hour after getting back on the trail at the ford, they reached the far side of the flat and entered some low hills, through which wound a small, permanent stream sparkling with the good water of high snows. A little bench on the north bank had been heavily browsed in times past, indicating it was a favorite stopping place, but there was ample new growth for the animals.

They slipped the packsaddles, turning them to dry where necessary. One by one the animals watered, then waded in where the bottom was good and rolled, washing off the accumulated adobe, which had dried and was pulling uncomfortably at the hair of their coats. They came out then, and rolled dry in the grass before beginning to graze.

Stanton thought the example was too good to ignore. He started a fire against later comfort, then stripped off his belt and emptied his pockets, stacking his belongings on a deadfall. In all of his clothes but boots and hat, he went upstream a little ways to clear water and dove in.

Seeing what he was up to, Jaime quickly followed suit. When as much of the outer mud as was possible had washed off, they took off garments one at a time and finished their laundry as best they could, hanging it on willows to dry. Stanton discovered that Jaime did not swim well and showed him the powerful scissors leg-kick that Bolo, the Carib, had taught him along with his Spanish. Jaime mastered it quickly and was delighted at his new-found prowess.

They dried their hides by the fire and dressed in clothing that was already little more than damp in this dry air. Stanton carefully cleaned and recharged his guns. Noting tracks on the creek bank, Jaime asked for the rifle and slipped off upstream. Stanton retrieved Sol Wetzel's inventory of the packs from his pile of belongings and opened it. It was a very businesslike document, every item pre-priced, and he realized that his own and the trader's combined interests in the packs totaled a very respectable justification for Royer's attempted banditry.

A rifle shot echoed from the course of the creek and Stanton put some larger wood on the fire to thicken the bed of coals. In a few minutes Jaime returned with a spike pronghorn, already drawn and flayed. He portioned off a meal and wrapped the rest in the hide for later use. As the meat roasted on his ramrod over the fire, Stanton studied the boy.

'How'd you come to join up with the wagons?' he asked.

'I didn't apurpose,' Jaime answered. 'It goes

back a ways, Mr. Stanton. Pa was trying to clear another planting patch and an old blackstrap hickory snag broke in two on the way down. The top part pinned him to the ground and broke him up pretty much. He got lung fever after and couldn't do much. Ma was failing, and when she died pa couldn't fend for us himself, so he farmed us out, mostly to uncles and cousins and such. All six of us. For board and needings. One ever which place. But pa needed some money, too, and a feller offered him forty dollars till I was sixteen. It seemed like a fair price, it wasn't only four years to go, and I couldn't get that kind of cash money quick for pa any other way, so him and me talked it over and reckoned it'd be all right. I wouldn't be starving and he'd have some of his needings, too.'

Stanton was aghast at the matter-of-fact account.

'Good God, that's plain child slavery!'

'No, I don't reckon,' Jaime said earnestly. 'Pa'd never cotton to nothing like that. He always said ever man is his own, even if he's black. Or white. Or Indian. No matter. He'd be bound to feel the same about his own young. It's just that we were mighty poor people. This was a kind of a business deal, like getting paid in advance for four years, and my keep and all besides. They made a paper about it and everybody signed it.'

'An indenture agreement?'

80

'Lord knows. Something like, I guess. And it worked out pretty well for quite awhile, too. I had no complaints. No harder than I'd been doing at home. This feller was real nice in his way. But he got drunk one night in St. Joe and lost me at cards to Bennett Royer. He tried to get me back the next day, but Royer wouldn't hear of it, even when he offered him more'n he paid pa. And only a little time left to go, too. So Royer took this job as wagonmaster and I had to come along.'

'Now you're running away from him.'

'You could say, I guess. Royer sure does. But not rightly. I turned sixteen two days after we got to Santa Fe. So that's the end. I figure from here on I'm working on my own. Mr. Wetzel figures the same. He says he'll stand for me if need be. But I don't know. Ben Royer's a mighty mean man to them that stand against him.'

Stanton leaned forward and turned the meat.

'I wouldn't worry about it,' he said. 'There are meaner, if that's what it takes. Royer'll find out. You stick with me, son.'

'I'd admire to,' Jaime answered with blunt earnestness.

Stanton smiled at him.

'Wetzel never did tell me your full name.'

'Jim. Jaime's just a joke of Mr. Wetzel's. Or the Spanish of it, one or the other. Jim Henry. Plain enough name, I guess. As pa always said, we're plain folks.'

'Good name, Henry. Famous one in my part of the country. But Jim—no, I like Jaime better.'

'I don't mind. I answer to either.' Jaime paused, then, uncertainly, 'You got any family, Mr. Stanton? You know—wife, young 'uns?'

'No,' Stanton said harshly. 'Memories. Not very pleasant ones. Ones to forget.'

He did not mean to be forbidding, but Jaime fell silent. There was no further exchange between them. They ate in silence, hobbled the animals, and turned into their blankets without goodnight.

## CHAPTER SIX

Stanton immediately liked Manuel Armijo. Despite his military title the general was very much the private citizen in bearing and dress. He was a heavily built man of medium height and with the florid complexion and hearty manner of a gentleman of appetites and good taste, freely exercised.

However large the total Armijo holdings in the area were, the residence to which they were directed was a small, irrigated table-crop farm on the bank of the Rio Grande, about six miles above Albuquerque. It supported what was on the outside quite a modest house. But once within there was everywhere rich evidence of gracious living. Stanton could see that Jaime was much impressed.

The general scanned Sol Wetzel's manifest of goods in the pack string, the trader's and Stanton's things separately totaled. Wetzel's efficiency, as well as his audacity and hard-headed pricing, seemed to amuse Armijo. Stanton suspected that considerable irrepressible rascality underlay the general's urbane exterior.

'If a Jew ever became a general,' Armijo said, tapping the manifest, 'God help the enemy and his own people as well! You understand, of course, that these prices are nothing short of banditry.'

'Dictates of business,' Stanton corrected firmly. 'There are difficulties between here and Santa Fe. It's expensive to overcome them.'

'You found that out, eh?' Armijo asked with a chuckle. 'Yes, I should think so. You and your'—he looked at Jaime and carefully chose the word for best effect—'your *segundo* must be remarkable men, if only for your luck. To bring so large a cargo of *yanqui* contraband through to us, contrary to the governor's orders. It has not been done before. Not while Albino Pérez has been in the palace.'

The general stretched his boots out in front of his chair and leaned his head back thoughtfully.

'You must understand,' he continued. 'They

83

say that all Spaniards are born to be kings and all Mexicans to be presidents. It's not always so far from the truth, if we are to be honest with ourselves. Our people are poor and uneducated. They need the help of a strong *rico*, a powerful *patrón*. Nowhere more so than here in *Nuevo Méjico*.

'Governor Pérez is in office by the power of the government and he tries always to strengthen the government to improve his own position. His own government, that is. In Santa Fe. Mexico City is far away. He taxes even the poorest. He taxes everything. The burden grows impossible for many, but he only adds more of his private guards and passes more laws. To him Santa Fe is everything. He cares nothing for the rest of the province.'

He shot a shrewd look at Stanton before continuing.

'I am different. Believe that, *Señor*. I speak for my friends, my neighbors, *mis niños*, down to the poorest. I speak by their will. I care nothing for government, for office. Believe that, too, if you will. I care only for New Mexico. All of it. All of the people. I want El Paso del Norte and Albuquerque, all of the pueblos, to have what Santa Fe has.

'I am what you would call a patriot, without meaning the same thing. I want the tax monies given back to the people instead of filling the treasure rooms in the *Palacio de los Gobernadores*. In time Mexico City will listen to me. Until then Albino Pérez must be my enemy, as I am surely his.'

The general drew himself erect again in his chair, his eyes alight with some secret relish.

'It pleases me to do what I can to displease him. It would please me to make some accommodation with you, if it is at all possible. But I will need until tomorrow. Come back then. Meanwhile, may I suggest you visit the great Duke of Albuquerque's fair namesake. One day it will be the great city of this province. You have the word of Manuel Armijo on that.'

He rose and escorted his callers to the door.

'Do not trouble yourself about your burros,' he added. 'My *mozos* will care for them. And the packs. *Hasta la mañana.*'

The door closed behind them and Stanton and Jaime walked out into the sun. They saw that their pack string had already been led away. As they mounted their horses, Jaime looked back at the house with obvious admiration.

'Didn't get too much of what he was saying, but I'm sure glad he's for us.'

'I hope he is,' Stanton answered.

*     *     *

As in Santa Fe, the heart of Albuquerque was a large plaza, dominated by an impressive old adobe church and an associated convent or monastery bracketing the two legs of one corner. Trade shops and business houses flanked most of the rest of the square. But here the similarity, except for the old Spanish colonial architecture, ended. Santa Fe was of the mountains to which it clung. Albuquerque was of the broad valley of the Rio Bravo del Norte, usually called the Rio Grande, and the brown stream itself skirted the town.

Sheep were everywhere on unfenced approaches, grazing wherever no crop was planted, fat and full-fleeced. Their sound was a part of the wind. Their dung paved every track with tiny, dark cobblestoning. The strong, steamy smell of baled sheared wool hung pungently over the town.

Carts were coming in from fields stretching away in both directions along the river, piled high with fresh green goods, sacked beans, and cobbed corn. The lowlands were rich here, more bountiful than Santa Fe's. There was a greater press of pace, the feeling of more commerce and work for a man's hands than in the mountain capitol.

Curious, Stanton tried some of the shops along the plaza. The wares they displayed were almost exclusively Mexican or of indifferent local manufacture and in inadequate supply. There were a few European imports, notably French and English cutlery and other edged steel, obviously come by the long, roundabout way via Mexico City. But many of the most common and useful items were totally missing.

Stanton realized that neither Wetzel nor General Armijo had been exaggerating. Governor Pérez's embargo on readily accessible Yankee goods from Santa Fe was working real hardship here. By extension, the potential of traffic and trade over the Santa Fe Trail—upon which so many trading houses in the States were speculating so hopefully—was being throttled to a mere trickle by the New Mexican governor's obstinacy.

It was, Stanton thought, a repetition of the situation in medieval Europe, when so many petty local lords and princes closed their private borders to exact import duties and transit tolls that the trade between nations and even neighboring cities came to a complete standstill—with subsequent widespread poverty and privation. If this was so, the winds of change were overdue. The lessons of history were precise in this regard. A persecuted people, even in so localized a situation, inevitably threw down their burdens, when they became intolerable, and turned upon their persecutors.

He knew that an educated man like Manuel Armijo must recognize this, and he thought that a shrewd one like Sol Wetzel did, too. Both were probably counting heavily upon it, each according to his own purpose. The time was fast approaching when Spencer Stanton must make his own decisions and consider his alliances, if he was to build the place he wanted

87

in this land.

While they were eating in a small place off the plaza, Jaime spotted a *casa de baño* across the street that offered hot water, soap, and a tub. Spurred by the boy's sheepish admission that it had been seven months and twelve hundred miles since he had bodywashed in earnest, Stanton bought them each a fresh shirt and underchange and they went in.

A fire burned under a large caldron in a courtyard at the rear. Several curtained adobe cubicles faced it, each containing a throne-like, high-backed tin tub. Stanton and Jaime were each provided with an almost translucent chunk of juniper-scented soap and were made to understand that when they were into their tubs, the water would be brought. Stanton was pleased to discover that his wounds had healed sufficiently to go without the none-too-clean bandaging. But his understanding of bath procedure must have been imperfect, for his water-carrier was a quite handsome, graying Indian woman, who entered his cubicle without ceremony, lugging a bucket each of cold and steaming water.

The woman was as disinterested and matter of fact about it as scrubbing a floor. She dumped the cold water over Stanton first, then sloshed in the hot. Feeling the resultant mix with a dipping finger, she seemed dissatisfied, for she returned with another steaming bucket and dumped it in as well.

Stanton roared protest, certain he was being seared to the navel, but the hot water continued to cascade in until the bucket was empty. Yelps from the next cubicle indicated Jaime was suffering a similar experience simultaneously. A Spanish voice called from another cubicle in reassurance.

The Indian woman was the best bath-mother Albuquerque had ever had. She knew the precise temperature to kill all body lice, nits, cankers, and bunions without taking the hide with them. Stanton thought there was some mention of crabs and French disease as well. A very old, very medicinal treatment long known to her people.

The water was still too damned hot for Stanton and he started to escape the torture. The Indian woman reappeared and thrust him back. She stood there sternly until his skin became accustomed to the unexpected heat and he subsided.

Twenty minutes later he was sufficiently soaped, rinsed, and resigned to allow her to reenter and towel him dry with a coarse, hand-woven cloth that very nearly finished what the hot water had not. But when it was done and he was dressed, he felt reassuringly clean and refreshed. Jaime, who had apparently had a similar attendant of his own, was in awe of the experience.

'She'd sure make somebody a hell of a mother!' he confided.

They went out into evening twilight and turned back toward the plaza. They found it packed and some kind of public event in progress. When they tried to push through the press to see what was going on, they were stopped by a cordon of determined men.

'*No pase,*' one ordered. '*Es para paisanos, solamente.* For countrymen. No foreigners.'

They fell back against a wall. Presently the shifting crowd provided an opening, through which Stanton could see a long, trestled table, piled high with assorted merchandise. Three or four men, obviously auctioneers, were doing a brisk business, disposing of their wares to the highest bidders in the noisy, spirited crowd. It reminded him of a stock auction at a back-county Virginia fair, and Stanton supposed it a similar local custom. Then Jaime, with perhaps a better view, caught his arm in outrage.

'Those are our packs they've got opened up and are selling off!' he yelled.

Stanton saw the boy was right. 'We'll see about that!' he yelled back. 'Come on!'

They started forward and immediately collided with the same cordon of sentries, effectively and warningly blocking their way. Stanton snapped his belt gun up.

'Open up or I'll blow you open,' he ordered.

'*Lo siento, señores,*' a voice behind him murmured softly, and he was knocked down by a deft blow to the head.

Hands disarmed him. Others dragged him

again to his feet, his arms clamped tightly behind him. Somebody retrieved his hat and clapped it back on his head. He saw that Jaime was also held helpless. The sentries surrounded them. Quietly, so that few if any of the crowd were aware of a disturbance, they were forced out of the plaza into an alleyway.

Their captors were good-natured and courteous enough. No undue force was used. But they made it plain further struggle was useless. Stanton and Jaime were hustled through the alley to the next street and along it a short distance to a stout, squat building with small barred windows high above eye level. A door was opened and they were thrust inside. A partition of bars divided the room. Beyond it were four or five cots. They were pushed into this cell and the gate clanged shut behind them. A man turned the key and pocketed it. Another took blankets and a candle from a locker and thrust them through the bars.

'*Que duerman bien, señores,*' he said, not without some amusement. And he followed his companions out to the street, closing the door behind them and leaving the prisoners alone.

'What did he say?' Jaime asked.

'Sleep tight,' Stanton answered.

Jaime looked disconsolately at their surroundings.

'Never been in jail before. I wonder for how long?'

'Ask General Armijo.'

'Yeah. He sure whipsawed us, didn't he? Real fine, upstanding feller.'

'A scholar and a gentleman,' Stanton agreed.

'In a pig's ass! Now what we going to do?'

'Take their advice,' Stanton said. He shook out a blanket. 'Sleep.'

*       *       *

Manuel Armijo received his angry callers in the *sala* of his modest house on the Rio Grande with a benign smile. Sol Wetzel's manifest for the goods the general had appropriated was on the table before him and he was just finishing counting out two heaps of money of all denominations from a small, stout chest.

'We do not have much in the way of hotels in Albuquerque, gentlemen,' he apologized. 'I trust you slept and breakfasted well and found your horses properly taken care of.'

Stanton let his hand drop to rest on the butt of his restored gun, but made no other answer. The general seemed hurt at the gesture.

'Surely you see the necessity,' he protested.

'Yesterday you said something about banditry,' Stanton said coldly. 'You could give lessons in spades.'

'I do what I have to do,' the general answered. 'We wanted those goods and supplies. We needed them. But how did I know what was a fair price to my people? Do I trust your friend Wetzel'—he tapped the manifest—'or you? No, I think not. But you have embarrassed Governor Pérez, so I am obliged to be fair to you as well. What better than to let the people of Albuquerque set their own prices? An auction to the highest bidder was the most sensible way to accomplish that. Do we still talk of banditry, *señor?*'

Stanton looked at Jaime. The boy was baffled.

'Is he saying what I think he's saying, Mr. Stanton?' Jaime asked.

'Keep talking,' Stanton told the general.

Armijo smiled. 'As it turns out, my countrymen were willing to pay a little more than even Sol Wetzel thought they would. *Mira*—'

He indicated the chest on the table. Stanton and Jaime moved forward and looked inside. A substantial amount of money was left within it. Armijo pushed the two piles of money counted out on the table toward Stanton.

'This, according to his manifest, is Wetzel's return for his shipment. This is yours. Each what you asked, down to the last *peso.* Your burros I have borrowed, as Wetzel borrowed them from their owners. Since they must go back to Santa Fe anyway, and the governor pays no attention to what enters Santa Fe, only what leaves it, I am venturing to send Wetzel a shipment of wool. Or you yourself can take it on consignment when it arrives. We have a

93

great surplus here. Perhaps you can find us a buyer in your country and send it east with one of the wagon trains.'

'That's for Wetzel,' Stanton said. '*This* is my country now. And I'm no trader.'

'You brought trade goods to Santa Fe. You came here to trade with me.'

'I freighted those goods to Santa Fe to move what capital I could salvage to New Mexico and at least make expenses on the way. I made the trip down here as a way to get back what was stolen from me and turn it into cash.'

'What, then, do you want?'

'Land.'

Armijo looked at Stanton thoughtfully.

'Yes,' he said. 'To be a part, you have to become a part. People who live on the land as we do know that. But you will be resisted. At every turn, I think. *Yanquis* are not loved. Particularly in Santa Fe.'

'They'll learn.'

'Perhaps,' the general agreed. 'In time. If you live. Make small friends, *amigo*. Many of them. Powerful ones are too few and too dangerous.'

Armijo rose and came from behind the table, indicating a large, leather saddlebag-like Mexican *mochila* near the door.

'Food for your return journey, from my own kitchen.'

'Wait a minute,' Stanton said. 'What about what's left in that money-box?'

94

He pointed at the chest on the table. Armijo smiled.

'Everyone will take a profit when it can be had, *señor*. My countrymen oversubscribed. It's only right the excess should remain here for their benefit. If Governor Pérez continues his policies, it may become necessary to do something about them. The people of your country understand that. Mine have the same rights. To defend a right takes money as well as men. You agree?'

Stanton met the general's eyes and returned his smile. It seemed a likely time to make his first investment in New Mexico.

'All right,' he said. 'On that basis. Call it my contribution, General.'

Armijo bowed slightly.

'With pleasure. It will be remembered.'

Stanton peeled up his shirt and pulled off his moneybelt. There was obviously not enough room in its pockets for the two heaps of currency on the table. Armijo saw the difficulty.

'Gold would be more convenient?'

'Much.'

The general excused himself and went into another room. He returned with a weighty leather pouch and counted out the equivalent of the currency in large, beautifully minted *pesos de oro*. Stanton transferred these to his belt without difficulty, reserving a pair of belt pockets for Wetzel's share. Armijo returned the reclaimed currency to the chest on the table. They moved to the door. Stanton picked up the *mochila* of food.

'Thanks for this.'

'*De nada*,' Armijo replied. He eyed Jaime. 'You do not have a pistol. Take this.' He lifted a belted, use-polished, small-bore double-barreled Spanish percussion from a wall peg and draped the belt over Jaime's shoulder. 'It is not the fine modern weapon that *Señor* Stanton carries, but it is an old friend. Like me, it has been around a time and ridden a few miles, but it still shoots very well.'

Jaime tried to stammer his gratitude but was too thunderstruck to succeed. Manuel Armijo clapped him on the back and shook Stanton's hand.

'*Bienviaje, amigos.*'

The door closed behind them and Stanton and Jaime went on to their horses with their gifts.

## CHAPTER SEVEN

Because Glorieta Pass, the route of the Santa Fe Trail through the Sangre de Cristos, emerged into the Rio Grande valley a few miles south of the City of the Holy Faith, the wagon road had to turn north to climb into the capitol. For that stretch the road paralleled at a decreasing distance the pack trail of the *Camino Real*, as it climbed up from the river. As soon as the lie of the land made it practical, Stanton turned off the pack trail and cut across toward the wagon road without approaching any closer to the city.

His purpose was twofold. For one, he knew that Royer or Lieutenant Montoya, or both, would have a watch stationed outside the town to intercept him, and he didn't want to risk encountering it on their terms. For the other, although he had not told the boy, he had no intention of riding back into Santa Fe with Jaime beside him. Not that he lacked confidence in his companion. Boys of sixteen had fought the redcoats on more than one occasion. But this was a private war and he would not needlessly risk anyone else.

They intersected the wagon road at a point where it skirted a small stream, about fifteen miles from the city. They watered the horses and refreshed themselves, then sat on a rock beside a stretch of sand. Stanton took a stick and began to trace on the smooth surface.

'Here's where this pass comes out of the mountains on the other side. The Trail turns north there. Here's where the Utes stole our horses. We thought that was a dry passage there, but it isn't. There's good water and grass in here, just a few miles west. That's where the Utes took me.'

'That's where your cattle are, too, isn't it?'

97

Jaime asked.

Stanton nodded.

'I don't think the Utes would be interested in just one horse and gun. I don't think they'll bother you. If they do, try to get hold of Chato. He's the boy we captured and turned loose. Or the girl, 'Mana. Once you cross the Canadian, the Trail's clear, and you've been over it.'

Stanton opened his shirt and reached into a pocket of the belt beneath. He fingered two hundred dollars in gold into his palm.

'There's enough of the general's grub in that *mochila* to get you a good way. This ought to cover the rest of it.'

He offered the coins to Jaime. The boy looked at him with hurt.

'What you trying to tell me? That we're splitting up?'

'You're going home. Back to find your father and your brothers and sisters.'

'And be another mouth to feed and a worry and fret again? If I ever go back, I'm going to be carrying a hell of a lot more gold than that!'

'I'll make it more. Double it, if that'll help.'

Jaime shook his head.

'I don't know what I done wrong, but you said to stick with you and that's what I'm going to do.'

'Not in Santa Fe, son,' Stanton said firmly. 'You haven't done anything wrong. It's just the way it is.'

'After Santa Fe, then?' the boy asked.

'Where are you going?'

Stanton indicated with his stick the spot on his crude map where 'Mana had nursed him back to health in an Indian brush shelter.

'If I'm lucky,' he added.

'When'll that be?'

'I don't know.'

'You're sure you won't let me stay with you?'

'I can't. Too risky for both of us. Want Bennett Royer to get hold of you again?'

Jaime stood up.

'We both got a chore to take care of and we're wasting time. You got business in Santa Fe and I got some stock to look to, up there in Ute country. Keeping wolves and bear and catamounts off. Keeping them bunched and picking up strays and moving them to the best grass and good water so's they'll fatten and prosper. They'll be there when you get there. So will I.'

Jaime started for his horse. Stanton overtook him at the animals.

'Think you can manage alone?'

'Look, Mr. Stanton, I told you how I've lived since I can remember. Lots of things is worse than being alone in open country at the best time of year. You say we got friends among the Indians. That's all I ask. Give me the grubsack and your rifle and I'll live like a king.'

Stanton grinned.

'I'll trade you for the general's pistol. A

99

spare might come in handy for what I've got to do.'

Jaime surrendered the Spanish belt gun without hesitation.

'Kill the sons of bitches,' he said earnestly. 'Kill them before they get another chance at you. I'll be waiting, and I want you to show up.'

He pulled abruptly to saddle and rode off down the trail without looking back. Stanton checked the loads of the Spanish pistol and tucked it into his underbelt in the small of his back, where his jacket would conceal it. Swinging up, he rode in the opposite direction for Santa Fe.

Stanton knew his best insurance was people. A lot of them. Laws could be subverted or a particular interpretation secured by bribe, threat, or agreement. Officials and enforcement officers could be controlled in the same fashion. The testimony of a few individuals could be fabricated or otherwise corrupted. But the real source of law and order—of justice itself, for that matter—was the ordinary citizen, acting in concert with others of his own kind. The more of them, the better.

This conviction did not spring from any undue personal belief in the honesty and integrity of the individual. Stanton had good enough reason to view this with doubt. It was merely that, in sufficient numbers, the ordinary citizen was unreachable, unavailable to temptation, and determined to conduct himself in the most favorable light possible in the presence of his fellows.

As Jaime had belatedly warned him on the way to Albuquerque, both Royer, with Hagen and Brock, and Lieutenant Montoya, with the governor's guards, would be best served by dealing with him in private and unseen. A simple repetition of Hagen's first attempt to kill him, this time guaranteed successful by numbers and official sanction. And justified because he was a fugitive thief resisting arrest—a legal concept familiar among Spanish-speaking people as *el ley de fuego*.

The money he carried would disappear. Enough of it would reach the governor or his public treasury to ease any curiosity or qualms that official might feel. And the fact that a portion of it belonged in fact to Sol Wetzel wasn't likely to trouble anybody but the unfortunate trader himself.

All other things being equal, Stanton supposed that the logical action was to approach the governor directly and publicly, thus compromising his official position between involvement and legal duty. It seemed likely that the official would be forced to respond differently in the open than he might in private, and that Royer's connection with the lieutenant of his personal guards could hardly be exhibited in public. He also thought that Wetzel, if forewarned, might be able to interest a few other local people of consequence in the justice of his fellow Yankee's claims.

But he had no idea what Wetzel's situation was now, since Don Felipe Peralta's letter to the governor had exposed the 'burglary' of the trader's storeroom all too plainly for what it was. And the governor's orders, if not the laws of the province, had been deliberately ignored. Comments by both Felipe Peralta and General Armijo about the government of Albino Pérez made any guess as to what the governor might do in the case of an invading *yanqui* extremely hazardous. Both had plainly warned Stanton he was a foreigner and in a foreign country.

He knew he had to think of his own stance, too, since he would have to live with it afterwards. The size of the shadow he was to cast. If he was to make a place in this country, as in any other, it would have to be as others saw him, not necessarily as he saw himself. He had trusted legally constituted authorities to enforce justice—according to the customs of society—once before when he had been injured, and he had lost. He had lost nearly all he possessed, all he held dear. He had lost the respect of others and his own as well. It was not a mistake to be repeated.

In the end he decided to do what he had known all along he must. It was the real reason that he had felt he could not afford to be hampered by Jaime Henry's fierce young loyalty and simple directness. If he was to ride back into Santa Fe at all, he must ride in tall in the saddle. He must set the whole community back on its heels. It was the only advantage he could count on—and then only if he was successful against disheartening odds.

Nearing the outskirts, before the curious could notice his passage, he turned from the rutted wagon road and cut casually across open plots, parallel to the little Rio Santa Fe until he came again to the ford that marked the actual beginning of the *Camino Real* to El Paso Del Norte and Mexico City. He turned his horse down it, away from Santa Fe, letting the animal set its own unhurried pace.

He knew Royer and Montoya would have their ambush or watch set not too far from the town. There was no need for more than sufficient distance to avoid attracting attention with the sound of gunfire. He also knew that there would be more than one or two men—so the job could be done quickly and to insure proper return of the money in his belt. And since they could not know precisely when he would be returning, it meant keeping a constant watch, changing shifts as necessary. Accordingly he was alert for any shelter or position that controlled the southern approach and could comfortably accommodate this kind of party.

Less than a mile from the ford across the Rio

Santa Fe and well within sight of town was a small, trailside tavern, or *cantina*, which had been dark the night he and Jaime had passed with their laden burros. Approach from town was partially obscured, since it came more or less from the rear, where a rude corral was attached to the hovel. But the trail up from Albuquerque was completely open from the other direction and visible for several miles across close-cropped, brown summer grass.

Two unsaddled horses were in the little corral. They were spiritless, poorly tended animals, and Stanton thought they probably belonged to the establishment, since it was hardly better kept. But four saddled mounts tied to a corral rail were another matter. They were well curried and equipped and ready for use at a moment's notice. Good horses, fast enough to overtake and run down any fugitive who had been long on the trail. And these horses, hardly normal trade for such a poor place at this hour of the day, were not racked in front, as would be usual, but hidden from sight of any approach from the south. He knew that here they waited for him.

Stanton held straight on, so as not to draw attention by deviating from the trail. He slumped somnolently in the saddle, as was the style of many of the local *paisanos*, and let his horse continue on unhurriedly. He had some hope of reaching the rear of the *cantina* unseen, but luck was against him. When he was still sixty or seventy yards away, a side door opened and one of Montoya's guards emerged, scratching himself and blinking in the sun. Stanton did not straighten or alter his plodding, deliberate approach. The guard moved to the front corner of the building and stood there for a moment or two, studying the empty trail to the south. Apparently satisfied that no one was yet coming from that direction, he turned back to the door and in so doing looked straight at the rider coming out from town.

It was a quirk of the human mind, not of the eye, that it often did not register the expected, the familiar, and the usual, even when fully visible, but rejected such sights as repetitious and useless information that would clutter the senses and occupy signal channels better reserved for more important, useful, or dangerous perceptions.

Stanton, closely watching from under his forward-slouching hatbrim, hoped this would be the case now. But he could not tell. The guard stopped and stared at him a long moment. Tension built. Then relief came. The man moved on to the rear corner of the *cantina*, turned his back to the approaching rider, and relieved himself against the corral. He must have been drinking beer in some quantity, for he puddled enormously and took forever to do it.

Presently, satisfied with his accomplishment

105

and tucking himself away as he moved, the guard returned to the side door and disappeared inside, apparently without giving any further thought to Stanton. Breathing a little easier, but with no assurance the man was not quietly alerting his companions, Stanton reined to the corral and put his horse among the others at the rail. Stepping around the guard's puddle, he eased to the rear corner of the *cantina* and along the side toward the door.

The horses in back indicated four men, with the proprietors of the place a further unknown quantity. If they were standing watches on and off, Navy style, some might be sleeping against their turn at duty. There was at least one of Montoya's guards. Probably two, one possibly the lieutenant himself. The other two he thought would be Yankees from the wagon train. Men who knew him by sight, which the governor's guards did not. Stanton smiled grimly to himself. That would not long be the case. In a very little while every man and woman in Santa Fe would know Spencer Stanton, or that the *yanqui* was dead.

He came to the door, but it was thickly planked and he could hear nothing within. The latch appeared to be a simple wooden affair with a leather lift-string protruding to the outside. He drew both guns from his belt, easing them to full cock, and planted his boot solidly at the latch. The door swung violently inward with a splintering of wood, and Stanton leaped with it.

An old man was dozing against a crude wooden cupboard, which apparently served as both pantry and bar. A fat woman with very full skirts and a jolly round face was bent over a kettle, craned out from a small beehive fireplace molded into the adobe of the walls in one corner. A guard with his boots off was stretched out on an adobe shelf, molded into the wall to one side of the fireplace. The guard who had come outside to relieve himself was on the opposite side of the single room, standing with a bowl of thick stew from the fireplace kettle in both hands, eating sloppily from it without benefit of utensils. In the center of the room Hagen and Brock occupied two chairs at a small, rickety table, a game in progress between them with a pack of greasy, dog-eared cards. There was no other furniture and no one else.

The old man and the woman went quickly to each other in mutual alarm, flattening fearfully against the wall without sound, their faces slack with the terror of the timid and frequently put upon. The guard who had been eating stood stupidly with the bowl in his hands, his open mouth full of food that slowly dribbled from it. The other guard, startled awake, sat up violently, but froze when he realized what was happening and did not swing his bare feet to the floor. Hagen and Brock both reached for pistols at their belts, kicking over their chairs and tumbling the table toward Stanton in a flurry of flying cards as they surged to their feet.

Hagen was the faster. Stanton shot him through the chest with one barrel of General Armijo's Spanish pistol. Hagen's belt gun, already in hand, fired into the packed dirt floor at a spot midway between them. Hagen buckled and collapsed over the weapon as it fell. Since Brock was slower and a lesser threat, Stanton gave him an instant in which to change his mind and reverse himself. But he seemed unwilling or unable to do so, and as his heavy-bore pistol continued its upswing, Stanton fired the other barrel of Armijo's double-bore, hitting Brock almost precisely where he had hit Hagen. Brock sprawled back against the fireplace, striking the back of his head with audible violence on the heat-hardened pan of the raised hearth.

Stanton leaped back against the wall beside the door, swinging the Navy Colt to cover the governor's two guards. It was not necessary. The one who had been eating suddenly dropped the bowl in his hands and was sick all over himself. The other sat wide-eyed on the adobe shelf, his bare feet still up, stiffly erect as though afraid to breathe. The fat woman huddled against the old man and began to whimper unintelligibly. Stanton put the Spanish pistol back in his belt.

'It's all right now, *mamasita*,' he told her

gently. 'It's all over now.' And to the old man, 'Bring around their horses and mine. All of them.'

The old man swallowed hard, nodded wordlessly, and tried to separate himself from the woman. She clung to him and they went out the door together.

'Get your boots on, *ándale!*' Stanton ordered the barefoot guard on the bench.

The man obeyed woodenly. Stanton found the guards' carbines leaning at the end of the cupboard and shook the priming from them. The woman and the old man came back to the door with the horses, all five of them. Stanton ordered the two guards to load Hagen and Brock across their saddles. He didn't know if either man was dead, and at this point he didn't give a damn. When the guards had finished he ordered them to mount their own horses and gestured to the old man to tie their hands behind their backs and their feet together under their girths. While this was being done he moved to the trembling woman.

'I'm sorry, *mamasita*,' he said. 'They would have killed me. You understand?'

She nodded dumbly.

'You'll remember how it happened if you are asked?'

She nodded again.

'You hear many things about *yanquis*. Some may be true. But don't believe them about this one. Only that I am a bad enemy but a good friend.'

He reached into his shirt and found two of Manuel Armijo's *pesos de oro*. He pressed them into her hand.

'For the damage. Believe me, if there had been any other way—'

The woman's eyes widened as she felt the weight of the coins She took a quick look in confirmation and smiled shyly.

'*Vaya con Dios, señor,*' she whispered. '*Buena suerte.*'

The old man handed Stanton the guards' carbines. He stuck them into their saddle scabbards in humiliating reversed position. Swinging up, he took the four leads from the old man and reined back up the *Camino Real*. At a small distance a little group of the curious had gathered uncertainly, alarmed by the sound of gunfire. He rode past with his captive cavalcade without looking either right or left. And he rode on into Sante Fe.


## CHAPTER EIGHT

Words of the *yanqui's* passage spread so swiftly through the town that as Stanton entered the plaza, trailed by an astonished, growing crowd, other awestruck queues flowed in from all directions. All seemed to understand his destination was the Palace of the Governors. A respectful lane opened for him. He saw in passing that Wetzel's store was closed, apparently unoccupied. There was no sign of Royer or Lieutenant Montoya. There was no challenge.

He halted at the palace portico and dismounted. Striding to the main door, he hammered loudly upon it with his pistol. It was opened by a *mozo*, who retreated into the interior, shouting alarm. Montoya appeared at a run, followed by several guards. They pulled up in the doorway at the sight of Stanton's pistol and the burdens on the horses behind him. Stanton indicated the two bound and disarmed guards.

'Are these your men, Lieutenant?' he demanded.

Montoya hesitated. The pistol decided him. He nodded.

'Arrest them. They tried to kill me at a *cantina* across the river on the Albuquerque trail.'

The pistol remained persuasive. Montoya wordlessly signaled his men to follow. Stanton stepped aside for them to pass. Their first concern was for the two Yankees belly-down across their saddles. A glance sufficed for Brock. Montoya called back from beside Hagen's horse.

'This one's still alive.'

'Too bad,' Stanton replied dispassionately. 'I'll only have to do it again. But do what you can for him.'

Montoya spoke to his men. They picked up the leads and moved off behind him, leaving Stanton's horse alone before the palace. Stanton entered the building. The frightened *mozo* who had summoned the guards lingered in the corridor. Stanton holstered his gun.

'Take me to the governor,' he ordered.

The servant obediently led the way past several closed doors to one that stood open. It was an anteroom, containing a paper-littered desk for a clerk, but it was unoccupied. The servant indicated a closed door in the opposite wall. Stanton opened it and entered without ceremony into what was more a spacious library than an office. The furniture was heavy and comfortable. There were shelves of leatherbound books, many of them very old. The room was dark and cool in contrast to the hot, bright sun of the plaza, and it exuded an aura of timelessness and tradition.

Albino Pérez stood at a small, barred window that gave onto the crowded square. He turned as Stanton entered. He was a slender, aristocratic, thin-faced man. His keen, cold eyes showed relish for the authority vested in him, but they betrayed no readable reaction to the scene he had just witnessed in the plaza. He sized Stanton up without greeting, closed the door to the anteroom, and sat down behind a large, orderly table, gesturing his caller to an opposing seat.

'You have a great deal of confidence,' he said.

'In justice—the law—the people,' Stanton admitted. He nodded toward the packed square—'when they have the facts.'

'Yes. Quite an entrance. It put my lieutenant in a difficult position out there. One of those men was dead. The other will also die?'

'If he doesn't this time, he sure as hell will the next.'

'Murder is punishable by the firing squad in this province.'

'Your lieutenant should have told Hagen and Brock that before they tried to kill me. And Bennett Royer—where's he?'

The governor shrugged.

'Send for him,' Stanton ordered. 'I have something to say to him that I want you to hear. And Sol Wetzel. It didn't look like he was at his store. He wouldn't have his door closed with that many people in the plaza.'

'He's in custody,' Pérez said. 'For investigation. A burglary the other night under rather peculiar circumstances.'

'You know what that was as well as I do. I want Wetzel and I want Royer.'

'I'm not accustomed to demands, *señor*.'

'As you said, rather peculiar circumstances.'

Pérez looked at Stanton a long moment and seemed to make up his mind.

'Very well. I don't know Royer's whereabouts. Doubtless he'll show himself when he learns you came directly here instead of looking for him. But I'll send for Wetzel if you insist.'

The governor tugged a cord against the wall. Stanton heard a bell ring in the anteroom. In a few moments an old man in white shirt and trousers and slapping sandals entered deferentially. Pérez gave the necessary orders and he withdrew. The governor returned his attention to Stanton.

'Understand, please, that you are a foreigner and you are in serious trouble. I am not pleased that you eluded Lieutenant Montoya and went on to Albuquerque against my orders.'

'I didn't elude Montoya. Royer convinced him it would be easier to take me on the way back with money than to run me down with a burro-train of merchandise.'

'You saw General Armijo?'

'He sold my goods for me.'

'Manuel Armijo is an enemy of the state.'

'They seem to think well enough of him in Albuquerque.'

'Illiterate farmers and sheepherders!' Pérez snorted. 'He intimidates them. To make a revolution—'

He broke off as the anteroom door opened and the white-clad clerk ushered Wetzel in.

'Am I glad to see you!' the trader told Stanton with relief. 'You hear rumors, but you never know. Specially in jail.'

'We'll try to straighten that out,' Stanton

114

said. He opened his shirt and freed his moneybelt. Sliding it out, he dropped it on the table before him. 'Not that I don't trust you, Wetzel, or you me, but I want His Excellency to witness this. We've nothing to hide. We disobeyed his orders only in that you didn't have capital to buy my merchandise and I had no other way of regaining possession of it. Here it is, right to the *peso*, according to that manifest you made out. And General Armijo siphoned off a commission for himself besides.'

Stanton opened the two belt pockets he had reserved for Wetzel's share of the returns and dumped Armijo's *pesos de oro* onto the table.

'Beautiful!' Wetzel breathed with compulsive admiration for the minted metal. 'But what's this out front the jailers were talking about. Armageddon, yet? Brock and Hagen both?'

'And a couple of his Excellency's guards to boot,' Stanton admitted with a slightly malicious smile at the governor. 'A little reception committee.'

'I was afraid of that,' Wetzel said. 'They knew you were alive and headed here. His Excellency had a letter and they found out. As soon as I tried to report our theft the next morning, they knew exactly what had happened and who was behind it.'

Stanton nodded. 'Jaime told me. After we were too far down the trail to do much about it.'

'You keep saying "they,"' Pérez cut in. 'Don't include me. Royer and Lieutenant Montoya, possibly. I'll know about that shortly. The men you shot. My two guards. But not the governor of the province. Pay me that respect. I knew nothing of this reception committee, as you call it. Only who you were and that you had ignored orders.'

'That we did,' Stanton admitted. He turned to the trader. 'We might as well face up to it. We took the chance. It looks like we'll have to pay for it.'

'How much?' Wetzel asked the governor with characteristic practicality.

'You mentioned a commission Manuel Armijo exacted. How much was that?'

'He didn't exactly give me a chance to count it,' Stanton replied wryly, 'but I'd guess it at about ten percent.'

'Very well, *señors*, that's what your fines will be. The state should benefit at least as much as a brigand.'

Wetzel started without protest to count out a tenth of the coin Stanton had spilled out for him. Stanton realized the quick-witted trader had gotten his message. Their profits from Albuquerque over Santa Fe were such that they could well afford the fine to end the matter. Stanton prepared to make a count of his own, but Pérez held up his hand in remonstrance.

'Later,' he said.

Wetzel pushed his counted coins toward the governor and pocketed the balance.

'You've been very lenient, Your Excellency,' he said with transparent ingratiation. 'I'm free to go now?'

'Ask my clerk to send for Lieutenant Montoya on your way out,' Pérez said with a nod of dismissal. 'I must detain *Señor* Stanton a few minutes on another matter.'

'See me when you can,' Wetzel told Stanton over his shoulder, and he hurried from the room, already fingering the gold in his pocket. The governor picked up the letter he had consulted on Stanton's entry.

'This letter is from Don Felipe Peralta. He tells me of your misfortune with your wagon train and some Indians, as he understands it. I presume the two *yanquis* you shot today are the ones you claim shot you?'

'One. The other was there, too. Both behind me.'

'We don't approve of taking the law into your own hands.'

'Even in self-defense?'

Pérez waved his hand impatiently, 'We'll return to the matter of the dead man presently.' He indicated the belt on the table between them. 'You have a great deal of money here?'

'Let's say a few thousand dollars.'

'I admire your caution.' Pérez smiled. 'I'm afraid it's justified. You see, I want this money. All of it.'

117

'You'll play hell getting it!'

'On the contrary. I already have it. Right here. You forget you're a *yanqui* under arrest and I am the governor. There's no question of who will prevail. Only if we can come to a sensible agreement.'

'You'll get from me exactly what you got from Sol Wetzel,' Stanton said flatly. 'Not a *peso* more.'

Pérez was untroubled. 'Wetzel was only guilty of smuggling contraband. Today you killed a man and another perhaps will die. That makes a difference. A very large difference. You'd better listen to what I have to say.'

Stanton realized he was boxed. With Royer and the two guards available and Hagen still possibly clinging to life, the governor could make any kind of case he wanted. And he could make it stick. He knew he was being sandbagged again. Just as ruthlessly and convincingly as he had been sandbagged by Belle and the bastard who had climbed into his bed. With no more justification. And for the same purpose—takeover of everything he owned.

'Go ahead,' he said. 'Talk.'

'That's better,' Pérez said. He returned to the letter. 'Felipe Peralta is a notable patriot. He's concerned over your purpose here. He fears it's land you're after and intend to get. A large tract known as the Corona Grant.'

'I crossed it, spent some time on it,' Stanton

118

admitted. 'Nothing on it. Nothing but country the way God made it. But it appealed to me. I asked about it. That's all. Tried to find out if it was open or who owned it. A woman, Peralta told me. No more. Said to inquire here.'

'Why didn't you?'

'Hell, when?' Stanton said bitterly. 'A few other little things. Trying to stay alive'—he thumped the moneybelt between them possessively—'trying to get my stolen property back.'

'You're still interested?'

'I didn't come all the way out here to turn into a trader or a half-assed smuggler or to rot in your goddamned jail!'

'You're not in a cell yet,' Pérez pointed out placidly. 'Records here are very old and there are a lot of them. Until I received Don Felipe's letter I was not aware that any old royal Spanish patents existed above Mora. That's border country, usually in the control of the Utes, as you discovered, and our people have always shown little interest in it. However, I had the archives researched.

'Don Felipe was right in what he told you. Title to the Corona Grant formerly was in the last of the old line, one Maria Dolores y Jesús Romana Ruíz de Herrera, a childless woman with no surviving family.'

Stanton's anger cooled as his interest grew.

'Was?' he asked. 'Then who holds the title now?'

The governor evaded the question.

'We've had these old royal grants, unimproved and even unoccupied for generations, before. When it comes to our attention that title has passed to a woman without a living spouse or other male of the line, or to any other heir judged incompetent to administer or improve the holding, the law allows the governor considerable authority. He can, at his discretion, return the grant to the public domain by forfeiture for redisposition to the greater benefit and productivity of the province.'

'That's confiscation,' Stanton protested.

'Not in practice. Unused land is valueless to anyone and pays no taxes. It is a burden to those to whom it has been passed. So there is no real loss or injustice. And if it can be made to produce by someone else, the state benefits. As I say, it is at the governor's discretion. Therefore I've had the proper orders entered. The legal title to the Corona Grant is now vested in the Province of New Mexico. That is to say, in me.'

Stanton was astonished. 'You're offering to sell it to me?'

'Many will disapprove,' Pérez said. 'Old Felipe Peralta, for one. Manuel Armijo will call me a devil's whore for it. Others, here and there, will say the same. They feel Mexico is for Mexicans. And they mean the land. Especially the land. But there is too much empty land in my province and two few *pesos* in my treasury. The Corona is a gap in our frontier. It should be closed. These are the things we in government must think about.'

Stanton sat looking at the man, thinking of General Armijo's complaints about him in Albuquerque and wondering just how many *pesos* from any source actually slipped through this governor's fingers into the provincial treasury. Pérez misunderstood his silence as indecision.

'I won't mislead you,' Pérez said. 'I can sell you land, but you won't buy friendship—even mine—or Felipe Peralta as a neighbor. I warn you of that. You are *yanqui*. Still, kings have had less. My clerk reckons the Corona at two hundred thousand of your acres, give or take a few thousand.'

Even the words had the sound of magnificence. Stanton thought of the vistas to which he had awakened in a brush Ute shelter on the bank of a quietly talking little stream. He thought of the smell of pine on the wind and the dapple of aspen in the morning sun on the higher slopes. He thought of his first view of his half-dead, trail-gaunted beeves on a shoulder of grass, renewing themselves on that rich graze. And the deep craving within him for something inviolably his alone. The place to build. The new beginning. Two hundred thousand virgin acres.

'How much?' he said.

121

The governor picked Stanton's moneybelt up from the table, balancing it in his hands, hefting it gently.

'About this weight in gold.'

Something within would not permit Stanton to let it be this easy.

'Less five hundred dollars. Living money.'

Pérez hefted the belt again. He hesitated a long time. Finally he opened it and counted out the named sum.

'I'll have the documents ready tomorrow,' he promised.

Spencer Stanton picked up the five hundred dollars. For a little less than eleven thousand he had bought an empire.

'Don't put that belt where you can't find it until you do,' he warned. At the door he turned. 'At that *cantina* today, Excellency— self-defense?'

'Self-defense. My guards will so testify. It will be so recorded.'


## CHAPTER NINE

The crowd that followed Stanton into the plaza had dispersed. The unhurried tempo of Santa Fe had resumed. As he picked up his horse and started across to Wetzel's store, Stanton saw Luis Montoya enter the square, obviously in response to the governor's summons. He thought this was a meeting that would not go particularly well with Montoya and, by extension, Bennett Royer. The thought pleased him. He paused, intending to pass the thought on, but Montoya saw him and ducked into a nearer door of the palace, far down the portico. Stanton shrugged and resumed. Montoya and Royer could wait.

Wetzel came quickly across the store to meet him when he entered. The trader's arms were spread wide as though for the Spanish *abrazo* of greeting. Actually it was to feel for the moneybelt beneath Stanton's shirt. When his hands found nothing Wetzel stepped back accusingly.

'He cleaned you!'

'Now why should he? He let you off pretty easy on that fine.'

'You make a little, lose a little. That's business. Dropping half of the profit to the government'—Wetzel shrugged—'beats giving it to the church. Or a woman. But you let him wipe you out!'

'No. We made a deal.'

Briefly Stanton filled the trader in on his transaction with the governor. Wetzel listened with increasing incredulity, and when Stanton finished he whistled with admiration.

'All I want to know is will it stick?' Stanton said. 'Is it legal?'

'As long as he's governor everything he does is legal,' Wetzel answered. 'He's made that plain enough to everybody, from the *paisanos* to the *hacendados*. Afterward, I don't know. Depends on who's next in line, I guess. But at that price, who cares? Possession is nine points of the law, even down here.'

'That's good news to me,' Stanton said approvingly. 'I've got some for you, too. At least I think it is, but I couldn't tell you over there. A message from General Armijo.'

Wetzel put his hands up in quick protest.

'Oh no he doesn't. No politics for me. I'm astraddle the fence and I'm going to stay there!'

'This is business. He's loading the burro string we used with raw wool. On consignment to you. He thinks you can send it back to the States on the return trains and sell it for his people at a better price than they can get in Mexico City. They'll split everything over the freight with you.'

Wetzel frowned thoughtfully, his merchant's mind at work.

'Maybe,' he said. 'Just maybe. Those wagons sure go back light. That's why more of them haven't risked the Trail. What can they load here? Nothing but a few furs, hides, beans, corn, and some Indian blankets once in a while. Wool's something else. Ought to be a good market. Even clear to England. The general's a thinking man.'

'And an ambitious one,' Stanton suggested.

'Wouldn't surprise me,' Wetzel agreed drily. 'Makes three of us, don't it? Where's the boy?

124

With the burros? Didn't want to ask in front of the governor. Probably would have wanted to fine him, too.'

'On the Corona. Waiting for me.'

'You two think you can get any kind of a crop in alone?'

'It's already in. My beeves.'

'Damn it, Stanton, you don't have beeves in this country. It's cattle. And you got to raise something else to even feed yourself. Every *paisano* in New Mexico knows that. I told you there's no beef market here.'

'So have several others,' Stanton admitted. 'But I didn't drive that stock out here to sell off what was left at the end of the Trail. I was looking all along for something like the Corona. Cow-kindly country where beef would prosper. Everybody on the wagons thought I was crazy, too. But I'm not. I never intended to peddle meat in Santa Fe. I've got my eye on the same market the general does for his Albuquerque wool.'

'The States?' Wetzel was incredulous. 'Across six hundred miles of the most troublesome trail freighters have tackled yet? You're letting that damned chunk of land the governor stuck you with go to your head!'

'I sure am,' Stanton agreed amiably, 'and I like it. I'll worry about how to get it to market when I've got a ranch laid out and beef to move. That won't be tomorrow. Right now I'll need a couple of packhorses, an outfit, and supplies for two for three or four months. Make it up for me. I have some other business to attend to.'

He started for the door and stopped as something arrested his attention.

'And a couple of nice ladies' dresses,' he added. 'Young ladies' dresses. Comes about to here'—he measured a spot on his shoulder and went onto the street, chuckling at Wetzel's astonished bafflement.

*     *     *

Because he no longer had any reason to avoid the comforts of the big inn, Stanton rode to La Fonda, put up his horse, and took a room. He freshened up and left Jaime's Spanish pistol there. There was a large tavern, reminiscent of those in the more westerly towns of the States, in La Fonda's corner on the plaza. He went in and ordered a drink. There was little trade and he concluded after a few minutes that the hour was too early for his purpose. Taking his change, he went by the back way he had used before to the livery where he had first put up in Santa Fe. He discovered that Wetzel had settled his account there when the trader had picked up his horse and gear while he waited in Wetzel's cellar. He crossed to the little *cocina* to pay for the meal he had been obliged to leave unpaid for want of local small coinage.

Finding he was hungry, he sat down again.

He was remembered and was well served. He ate leisurely, listening to the quiet flow of talk around him. He knew he was also being recognized from his ride in with his prisoners, earlier in the day, and that considerable excitement persisted about that. He could feel a lively curiosity about him, but he was not put upon in this courteous little room. When his hunger was satisfied and he considered enough time had passed, he paid his bill with suitable change and left.

The sun was low and Santa Fe's promenade of the walks and the plaza had begun, mostly the very young and the elderly at this early hour of the evening. Everywhere the best and cleanest attire was evident, with the small fry conscientiously aping their elders in manners and custom, even to the shy coquetry of even very small girls. Stanton found this miniaturized repetition of the strolling scenes he had been a part of before most pleasant. It was so serious and mannerly, compared to the raucous rowdiness of evening street play in other towns he remembered. He was aware of lively curiosity about him here, too, but it was voiceless and did not intrude.

Broad shutters, which had earlier closed the wide, glassless windows of the La Fonda tavern against the sun on the plaza side, had now been turned back so that those within could watch the passing parade in the square and vice versa. Near one of them Stanton found a small corner table from which he could see both the interior and the promenaders.

In a few minutes the pair of governor's guards who had been at the little *cantina* on the Albuquerque trail came in and took another table, some distance away, without seeing him. They were in fresh uniforms and good spirits, so Stanton assumed any discipline they had received had been light. Presently two girls left the promenaders and offered to join them. The offer was declined with obvious regret. Stanton continued to watch with growing interest.

Montoya entered, passing the girls as they returned to the plaza. His head turned after them but they ignored his attention as though he was nonexistent. At first Stanton was not sure of identification. The lieutenant was not in uniform and his black mood was plain across the room. He flopped down in a chair at the guards' table and commenced an angry harangue with them. Both tried to remonstrate with him, but Montoya only seemed to grow angrier.

Finally Bennett Royer appeared from the body of La Fonda itself. He had been drinking and was in no better a mood than Montoya. The two girls passed again in the plaza. The two guards tried to rise and quit their companions but were thrust back into their seats by Royer and Montoya. Stanton caught the eyes of the passing girls and signaled. They turned uncertainly in at the next doorway and approached uneasily. He rose to meet them.

'*Perdónenme, señoritas,*' he said, 'but I could not help noticing.' He gestured to a passing waiter. 'I have finished my drink and was just leaving. You're welcome to my table. If you will have a *chocolate*, I'll try to get your friends out of their difficulty.'

Their eyes followed his to the guards' table. They looked back at Stanton. He saw that he did indeed have a reputation of sorts in Santa Fe this evening.

'*Porqué no?*' one asked with a charming little shrug. 'Why not?'

They both giggled and sat demurely in the seats Stanton held out for them. The waiter brought two dainty cups of *chocolate*. Stanton paid him and moved toward the other table. Montoya saw him coming and surged up out of his seat. Royer dragged him back down. Stanton came up and smiled down at the uneasy guards.

'The ladies are waiting, gentlemen.'

Both showed startled relief, if not out-and-out gratitude. They scraped back their chairs and hastily left. Royer glared after them.

'Back-stabbing, chicken-shit bastards,' he spat. Stanton dropped easily into one of the empty seats. Royer looked at him. 'You'd lay snowballs for eggs, wouldn't you? You're behind this, damn your guts.'

'Not behind, Royer. What I do to a man, I do to his face. What are you talking about?'

'Luis here, drummed out of the guards and fined the three months back pay he's owed. And I'm run out of Mexico. Me and Hagen both, soon's he's fit to ride a wagon. If he don't die first.' Royer scowled at the two guards, sitting happily at Stanton's table with the two giggling girls. 'And them off clean, innocent as bare-assed babies!'

'Because they signed affidavits that you killed in self-defense.'

Montoya's voice was silken but vibrating like a taut wire with outrage and bitterness.

'Well,' Stanton said. 'It appears Governor Pérez is as good as his word. I must admit I had some doubts about that.'

'If I owe you thanks for this disgrace, it's a debt I'll pay in full. You have a Montoya's word on that.'

'There's another you'll pay first,' Stanton countered calmly. 'Both of you. Now. A new freight wagon and a six-up team you got the governor to issue you an order to sell.'

Royer and Montoya looked at each other. Stanton saw the signal pass. He smiled.

'There's a Navy Colt under this table, ready to drill a thirty-six caliber hole through a couple of bellybuttons before either one of you can move. I'd as soon fill a full house today as stand on a pair.'

The two looked at each other again. The signal was reluctantly countermanded.

'That was weeks ago,' Royer protested.

130

'Hell, there's not much left. That order to sell cost something. A tax for the governor.' He indicated the two young guards at the other table. 'They got plenty, too.'

'We'll see,' Stanton said. 'Cough up. But be careful.'

Very slowly Royer began to empty a pocket. He looked about, furious that this could be happening so quietly among so many people, attracting no attention. Stanton's eyes warned him. Montoya soon hit bottom. Stanton expected that. With Royer dealing out shares, the Mexican would have received little to begin with. Presently Royer also put both hands back on the table top. Stanton eyed the money stacked between the hands and shook his head.

'Try again.'

Royer's hand went reluctantly to an unexplored pocket and added more to the heap.

'That's better,' Stanton said. 'Now Brock and Hagen too. You'd have stripped them as soon as you could get to their bodies.'

'Damn it, Stanton, some of that's our money, my money! Wages from the train and what we had on us.'

'Today it's all mine.'

Royer reached into his shirt and angrily flung a bound buckskin pouch on top of the rest. Stanton scraped the pile together and dumped it into his jacket pocket. As he stood up, Royer saw the Navy Colt was still in its holster.

'You son of a bitch,' he said, 'you never even had us covered!'

'Not necessary. Too much danger in such a crowded room.'

Royer stood up and started away. Stanton stopped him.

'Royer—my trunks. You can keep the outfit you're wearing.'

The man rocked in fury on the balls of his feet for a moment.

'You staying here?'

Stanton nodded.

'I'll have them sent to your goddamn room.'

The two hurried angrily away and disappeared into the inn. Stanton followed more leisurely and had a drink at the bar. He thought he would relish a night's sleep in a good bed for a change. It might be a long time before he had another.

\* \* \*

The packhorses were standing hipshot in the cool of morning shadow in the alley behind Wetzel's storeroom when Stanton arrived. A hostler was just finishing lashing up the packs. Wetzel handed Stanton a bill.

'I figured you'd want an early start,' he said. 'Everything's listed. Better check it over to see if there's anything else you need.'

Stanton scanned the list without much

132

attention. He knew the little trader had a far better idea about what his requirements might be in this country than he did at this stage of the game. This would not always be so, but in the beginning—He drew Wetzel back inside and paid him the bill. He then handed him an envelope containing the rest of the five hundred dollars he had salvaged from the governor and the debts he had collected at La Fonda during promenade the evening before.

'Keep this for me,' he said. 'I'll have no use for it up there. Not this season, anyway. It'd just get in the way. Somebody might get a notion to borrow it if I had to keep it by me.'

Wetzel saw how much there was and his eyes widened.

'Not bad for a man that was clean the last time I saw him!'

'Some debtors cooperated.'

'Royer?'

'Montoya chipped in a little, too. And Hagen and Brock, posthumously, I guess you could say.'

'Royer won't let you get away with it. Not after the way everything else has worked out for him.'

'See why I need a banker? Somebody I can trust. So does Santa Fe. That's something we'll have to talk about one of these days.'

'Hell, man,' Wetzel protested, 'I can't just bury it in the cellar. Goes clean against whatever conscience I've got. Money not

133

working's a crime against God and man.'

Stanton grinned at him.

'Put it into Albuquerque wool then. Make yourself something from it, too. You complain about no working capital. Just so I can draw if I need a little.'

He stepped back into the alley and mounted, then remembered.

'Some trunks in my room at La Fonda. Can I store them here until I get a roof over my head again?'

'For free,' Wetzel grinned back from the doorway. 'I'll have them brought right over.'

'Thanks, *amigo. Hasta luego*—'

Stanton picked up his packhorse leads and rode around into the plaza. The square was empty, but he did not have to dismount before the *Palacio de los Gobernadores*. In spite of the early hour, the governor's clerk saw him coming and hurried out under the portico to hand him up an oilskin packet.

'The documents are all there, *Señor*.' The clerk hesitated. 'The governor asked me to say that he does not think it would be wise to pay a visit to Rancho Mora at this time.'

Stanton smiled. 'Thank His Excellency. Tell him that I couldn't agree with him more.'

The clerk nodded and reentered the palace. Stanton rode out of the plaza and turned his string toward the mountains.

# CHAPTER TEN

As he rode, Stanton assessed his position. He knew he was not finished with Bennett Royer. Wetzel had been right about that. He also realized that Royer really had little choice. It seemed likely that Luis Montoya would continue to throw in with the former wagonmaster, if only to carry out his personal threat of retaliation. Hagen was apparently still alive and might survive to rejoin Royer some time later, but he did not figure in the present situation.

Stanton knew he had forced Royer's and Montoya's hands at the La Fonda tavern. He had cleaned them out of funds. The amount he had salvaged from them, although less than the value of his appropriated wagon and teams, assured him of that. Pérez, for personal and political reasons, was certain to prevent any word of the sale of the Corona leaking from his office. Royer and Montoya would therefore assume that Stanton was still in possession of not only what he had taken from them but the gold he had brought back from Albuquerque as well. They would unquestionably come after it.

Royer's banishment from Mexico would not greatly hamper him. It primarily meant banishment from Santa Fe, since Pérez seemed disinterested in or incapable of extending his physical control much beyond the capitol itself. General Armijo's open and militarily uncontested opposition in the lower Rio Grande valley was proof of that. Once out of the vicinity of Santa Fe and the notice of the governor, Royer would, with reasonable care, be as much a free agent as any other Yankee in the province.

At the La Fonda Stanton had given no hint of his departure from town, deliberately leaving his trunks until he was on his way. But it was impossible to leave a town the size of Santa Fe without some notice. In a few hours Royer and Montoya would discover he was gone, presumably carrying his money with him. Perhaps back to the States. They would be quick to follow. His best advantage was that they could not know his actual destination. Only the governor's office and Sol Wetzel knew of the Corona. Only the trader knew that the remnants of his cattle, abandoned by the wagon train, were now on Corona grass.

He needed, then, to travel where he would leave no trail and where few, if any, would note his passage. For this reason he had shunned the ruts of the wagon trail over Glorieta Pass, the route to which he had directed Jaime Henry, and turned directly into the mountains.

North and east of Santa Fe, near at hand and almost on crow-flight to Mora, the highest and most massive peaks of the Sangre de

Cristos shut off the sky. Southward, below Glorieta, they taper away into the broad, more gentle undulations that separate them from the Sandías, back of Albuquerque. But northeastward, from Truchas Peak to the Cimarron, they are one of the most concentrated and formidable mountain barriers in the world, forming an almost impenetrable wilderness since primordial times. And the rise into them on their southwest approach is breathtakingly abrupt and frequently impassable. This was Stanton's route.

There were a few small plots, houses, and scattered shanties for the first two or three miles, lifting away from the town. Then marks of mankind fell away completely. By noon he had ascended through the thin, gray, dusty green of pinon and desert cedar to a steep, treeless upland of grass and occasional low, brushy clumps of stunted alder and willow. There were no streams here. Water was subsurface, rushing down the granite bones of the mountain beneath the overlying sod, so that the hoofs of his horses sucked in low places and water puddled in their tracks. The sun was hot and the horses sweated copiously with the steady, relentless climb, but the downslope wind was so cool that Stanton put his jacket back on for comfort.

There was no place ahead to look but up. The mountains grew greater as he climbed.

Slowly the line of big timber, dappled with the light, bright green of aspen groves, moved down toward him. But the gaunt, fierce, naked rock of the high peaks beyond thrust ever higher.

Delicate, low-growing flowers, unlike any Stanton had ever seen, began to appear singly and in little patches, mingled with the grass. The slope took on a faint, varying sheen of their pastel colors. A natural basin of stone, thrusting through the spongy sod, momentarily trapped rushing water, surfacing it in a little pool. He dismounted and knelt to thrust his face into it, drinking thirstily, as an animal would. It was icy cold and tasted like no other water ever had.

There were game tracks around the brink that he could not identify but that he thought might be mountain sheep or goats. While his horses watered he looked back the way he had come. He had been traveling steadily for half a day, but Santa Fe was still in plain sight, its adobes separating themselves by their shadows from the adobe color of the lower foothills. But it was far, far below.

Far beyond the town, in the blue void of the broad valley, the silver ribbon of the Rio Grande was easily traceable from where it emerged from the red slot of its canyon to a vanishing point at the foot of the distant Sandías, where Albuquerque lay. Westward the red and purple land slanted into an infinity of distance, an occasional mesa or butte or cone standing sentinel to the miles. Nowhere, from the utmost distance to his feet, was there a trace of pursuit.

Stanton smiled. He had thought that if he struck into the mountains, they would not follow—could not, in fact. He had thought they would take the wagon trail for its faster travel, knowing that he would have to come out to it on the other side, where they would be waiting. He walked his horses for a quarter of an hour after they had watered, leading them on foot. When he pulled back to saddle he found himself breathing heavily in the thinning air.

About two o'clock he entered a belt of big timber and shortly encountered a thickly grown slope that steepened until he couldn't ask the horses to take it any longer. The growth was so thick and the slope so steep that it was impossible to see far enough to choose the best alternate route. He settled for circling along the sidehill, unwilling to give up any of the altitude he had gained. In half an hour he heard water below. He continued on at his own level and a creek rose rapidly to meet him.

He turned gratefully up the stream, assuming water grade would not tax his tiring horses too much. But presently he became aware of a muted roar ahead that was increasing in volume. In a few more minutes he emerged from the timber into a small meadow about a pool, into which the creek plunged from a sheer ledge high above in a spectacular, free-falling cascade. The mountains thrust in oppressively from all sides except the direction from which he had come. He realized he had reached the headwall of a box canyon that effectively blocked further progress.

A few hours of daylight remained, but the meadow was so beautiful that Stanton was reluctant to turn back for fear of finding an inferior campsite when failing light forced a halt. He was, he reminded himself, in no hurry. Once he thought life had ended. Now it stretched a long way ahead. He slipped the saddles, rubbed the horses down with handfuls of grass, and hobbled them to browse. Setting about to pitch his first camp with the outfit Sol Wetzel had assembled for him, he came upon the ash of an old fire. How recent, he did not know.

A circuit of the pool at the foot of the falls showed fresh game tracks of every description, but there were no axe-marks on the deadfalls he gathered for his fire. As he shaped a rock basin for his fuel, he uncovered a worn rag of buckskin to which a few beads yet clung. He smiled, remembering 'Mana's instructions for finding the Indian trail that would lead him to Don Felipe Peralta's Rancho Mora. First, game tracks. Then, the game's trail. After that, other signs for which to look.

He thought in the morning, with a little luck,

he might be able to find a way out of this box canyon without having to backtrack or lose precious altitude—so hard to gain in such rough and unpredictable country.

*     *     *

After a full night's sleep, deepened by content and lulled by the ceaseless roar of the falls, Stanton breakfasted in the dark. By first light—that part of the day that belonged to him—his camp was struck and his packs made up. Leaving his horses hobbled to continue feeding, he set out on foot. In the narrow confines of the little box canyon, he did not have far to go.

Within a few rods he came upon a recognizable game trail leading away from the pool at the foot of the falls. It slanted in a downstream direction up the opposite sidewall to the one he had made his approach along the previous afternoon. It climbed steeply, but always seeking the easiest going. About halfway up it reversed direction to join an even more plainly marked trail climbing upstream from below and steeply slanted to top the head-wall of the canyon.

The mountain people, 'Mana had said, did not use pack animals. They had no use for any stock but dogs and war ponies. But they made the ponies earn their keep when a band was on the move. They used travois, two sapling poles

141

like the shafts on a single-horse buggy or cart. Their gear was carried lashed on a hide stretched between the two poles, and the butt-ends dragged on the ground in lieu of wheels.

There in the pine-needle-sifted track that the game trail joined was the unmistakable sign of Indian passage. A center path cut by the hoofs of the ponies and, equidistant on either side, the furrow gouged by the dragging butts of travois poles. 'Mana had said mountain people always followed the trails cut by game. They lived on game and needed meat at every camp. But they also knew that in the mountains, where the going was so tortuous, game always found the easiest going.

As with the fire ashes below, Stanton could not tell how recently this triple trail had been used. But certainly it had been used many times. He thought, however, by the indistinct edges of the impressions and a drift of needles over them, that the last passage had been some time ago. He went back to his camp and saddled up.

\*     \*     \*

After the hard pull up over the headwall of the box canyon, the Indian trail followed the floor of a relatively level, narrow, meadow-like alpine valley, partially flooded by innumerable beaver dams. The sharp reports as the tails of these wary animals slapped the surfaces of their ponds in signals of intrusion echoed against the higher peaks like gunshots.

However, a species of white-tailed deer, rather larger animals than Stanton had somehow anticipated, lay everywhere back from the stream in aspen shade, waiting for the shadows to lengthen. They paid little or no attention to the intruder and his laden horses. Stanton realized they had probably never been hunted with firearms. He had nearly two hundred in sight at one time by saddle count and he supposed many more were deeper in the silver-trunked aspen groves.

Further on brambly thickets overgrew the banks of the narrowing stream. Stanton's horses sensed something and began to dance nervously. He heard snorting and the berry-laden brambles threshed. A huge black bear sow and two half-grown cubs came out of the thicket. They, too, paid no attention to the intruder, passing within fifty yards of where Stanton was fighting his trembling, frightened horses. The bears crossed a patch of belly-high grass and disappeared into the timber, but it was half an hour before Stanton could calm the horses.

The dwindling valley threaded around the base of a stark, forbidding mountain and pinched out between two more great peaks. Stanton looked up at the saddle between them, far above the snowbanked timberline, which he realized must be the pass by which the

Indian trail reached the northeast slope. He could not see the trail up there, but travois poles did not wear away granite as they did lowland earth and there was no other way to go.

In spite of the grand scale and the height, he was growing accustomed to the paradoxes of dimension here. He knew the remaining climb was not a great distance over the ground. Nearly half of the day remained and he decided to go for the top.

Six hours later afoot, man and horses both heaving, night rose swiftly out of the deeply trenched valleys and canyons below, overtaking them on a bare, almost impossibly steep rock-field of enormous boulders, about half-way between timberline and the saddle between the two peaks. Stanton realized he could not get back to adequate shelter below timberline before dark. He was sure descending would be at least as difficult as the climb had been. And obviously he couldn't go on to the summit of the pass.

With no other choice, he found a small level space behind a huge rock that promised some shelter from the increasingly icy wind. There was snow above and a trickle of water flowed past. He unsaddled the horses and rubbed them down with a canvas pack-cover. He rigged a jury picket line and tied them to it, unwilling to risk hobbles on this uneven footing, where they might fall or snap a leg. It was all he could do for the animals.

Fireless and supperless, Stanton wrapped himself in a blanket and another tarp and sat leaning against the rock to wait it out. The wind turned even colder and continued to rise, coming at times in wild, buffeting gusts that moaned through the rock-field like some great, tormented animal. Stanton was soon chilled to the bone and could not sleep. The horses fared no better. They slid their ties along the picket line to lean against each other for warmth, and throughout the night they stamped and snorted protest.

It remained very cold, but in time the wind gradually dropped to a whisper and then was still, leaving a silence so vast that it seemed to create sound of its own. Somewhere, up on one of the peaks, a rock-fall clattered alarmingly, echoing back and forth like thunder until it slowly diminished to nothing. Some innate sense told Stanton it was a mere trickle of loosened rubble on the flank of the mountain, probably shifting no more than a few yards, but in the silent dark it had the impact of an avalanche.

Light came slowly on this dark side of the mountain. When there was enough to define the peaks and the saddle between them, Stanton forced himself to his numbed feet and saddled the horses. The animals were docile enough, anxious to resume their burdens and warm themselves with work, but his hands

145

were so cold and clumsy that he had trouble even threading the cinches through their D-rings, and his wounds had stiffened painfully. He walked beside his mount, letting the horse pick its own way for the trailing packhorses, and with his near hand clung to the horn of the saddle to steady himself until feeling returned to his feet. Then he resumed the lead.

The summit of the pass came abruptly. A small, almost unnoticed rock cairn marked it. The sun met him there, already lighting and warming the whole eastern slope. The mountains here descended less violently than on the Santa Fe side, breaking up into a decreasing turbulence of cascading lesser peaks and subsequent foothills, interlaced with frequent canyons carrying water out onto the grass, blueing off into the distance. From this vantage Spencer Stanton saw his domain for the second time, an expanse of blue land at the bottom of the world, slowly turning rosy with the rising sun.

Other small cairns, he discovered, marked the Indian trail at infrequent, strategic intervals to timberline. He supposed the ascent through the rock-fields had been marked the same way, if he had known what to look for. His practical nature was annoyed by the oversight. But a man gained new skills only by learning, and as he had been told so often since first seeing the Corona, he was still a *yanqui*.

A vertical thousand feet below timberline, at

the edge of a small, spongy meadow, cut by a little stream, he halted to build a fire, eat breakfast, and stretch out on the grass in the warming sun while the horses watered and fed. They were as reluctant to move on as he was himself, but for what was actually the first time in his life, he was headed home. At least as he had always understood the meaning of the word 'home.' And the impatience of anticipation was driving him harder by the hour.

The Indian trail was again well marked by travois poles, the grade generally gentle, and the horses picked up with the easier going. Stanton held on till dusk and spent the night in the mouth of a small canyon he judged to be twenty-five or thirty miles north of Peralta's Rancho Mora. Far enough, he thought, to avoid contact with the testy old don or his men.

In the morning, hardly a mile out onto the grass from his camp, the trail he had followed over the mountains joined the one by which 'Mana had sent him to the Peralta place on the way to Santa Fe. He turned eagerly north on this and, without stopping at noon, came two hours before sunset into the valley below the brush Ute shelter from which he had first looked over this land.

His cattle were not on the slopes where he had last seen them grazing. There was some sign of them along the stream, but the droppings were dry and the tracks in the mud long filled with water and disintegrating. They had not watered here for days. And beeves did not stray from good feed. They had to be moved. If they were, there had to be somebody to move them, and a reason. A vague uneasiness came over him. He rode on to the shelter.

It was obvious from a distance that no one was there. When he rode in it appeared that nothing had been touched, including the ashes of his last fire. Everything was as he had left it. This also troubled him. He was not worried about Jaime. His own route over the mountains cut off many miles from the track of the Santa Fe Trail. His business in Santa Fe had taken less time than he feared it might. He had been only a day behind the boy in leaving the capitol. Jaime would be along. He was confident. But 'Mana—

He laughed at himself. Somehow he had expected her to be here. That was it. Not the cattle. They could be found. He had expected the girl to be here. Waiting. Eager for his return. Eager for his news. Eager for him. Without an advance message. Without knowing what had happened in Santa Fe. Without knowing he was coming back or that he ever would. Without expectation. Yet he expected her.

The hell with that. It was a fantasy of his own manufacture and he knew it. Simply being too long without a woman. Yet he had not been tempted by the admiring eyes of the *señoritas* in Santa Fe. Fantasy—nevertheless a deep feeling of disappointment persisted as he unsaddled his animals and turned them out on hobbles.

On a whim, humoring the mood, he opened one pack but broke out only food for supper and a couple of blankets, leaving the rest of his outfit undisturbed. He'd celebrate this homecoming by using the simple, familiar brush shelter for the night. Time enough to set up a proper permanent camp in the morning. Maybe he would have the same dream as before.


## CHAPTER ELEVEN

His meal finished before the long shadows of the mountains reached out across the grass to him, Stanton sat idly before the fire, desultorily tossing twigs of green from nearby brush and handfuls of grass onto the embers so that a tall, slender column of white smoke rose high against the blue in the motionless evening air. He tired of this only when such a signal could no longer be seen in the deepening twilight. With a saddle-axe from the opened pack he went into the brush and cut several armloads of dry growth. When the pile beside the fire satisfied him, he sat down in front of it again and fed the flames until the darkness retreated a score of yards. He knew that from this vantage it would be a beacon visible for miles in virtually every direction. So the fantasy still persisted, and in this quiet hour he was unwilling to dispel it.

Stanton did not know how long it had been, but the pile of fuel was nearly exhausted when he stiffened suddenly, excitement racing through him as he caught the sound of a horse out on the grass, approaching unhobbled. He jumped up and hurried in welcome toward the sound to the edge of the firelight. But it was not one horse that emerged from the darkness. There were four. And the rider of the first was Abelardo, the *segundo* at Rancho Mora. With him were three heavily armed *vaqueros*. They rode silently past Stanton to the fire. Curious and uneasy, he followed. Abelardo dismounted, surveyed the laden packsaddles, and faced Stanton.

'So it is you, *yanqui*,' he said harshly. 'The *patrón* was right about you. You have come back. And to stay, it seems. Why?'

Stanton did not like his tone.

'If it's any of your business, which it isn't, some stock of mine was abandoned by the wagon train I was with when I was shot. Somewhere near here. I hope to find them.'

The *segundo* nodded and smiled at his companions, as though in complete confirmation of their suspicions.

'We saw their sign along the creek. But they

150

are not there now. They are gone.'

'Strayed,' Stanton said. 'But not far. They wouldn't and couldn't. They shouldn't be hard to find. As you see, I got here just ahead of sunset.'

'The *patrón* is missing two of his finest young bulls,' Abelardo said. 'As you say, such animals do not stray far on their own. We were sent to find them. The tracks of your horses have been with theirs all the way. Where did you hide them?'

'You read the book wrong, my friend,' Stanton protested. 'I'm hardly a cattle thief. I came over the mountains from Santa Fe by an Indian trail that cuts across the one you followed here nearly thirty miles north of your rancho.'

Abelardo looked incredulous.

'El Cumbre?' he asked derisively. 'You crossed El Cumbre—a *yanqui?*'

He laughed derisively and his companions joined in, as at a great joke.

'You're quick to use what you hear. I'll give you credit for that. But learn what else you should have heard about El Cumbre in Santa Fe. Mine is an old family and I know. Aside from *indios* there haven't been ten men in the history of *Nuevo Méjico* who have ever crossed El Cumbre, let alone packhorses loaded down like yours. Even the Indians never try it unless they've been on a raid or thieving and are running for their lives.'

He turned to his *vaqueros*. They gradually moved closer.

'We've found who took the bulls, all right, *compañeros*,' he said with satisfaction. 'As he says, they must be close—with his strays.'

'Hell,' Stanton complained angrily, 'use your damned head! What kind of a thief would I be to light up the whole damned countryside to show where I am?'

'*Quién sabe?*' Abelardo shrugged imperturbably. 'All *yanquis* are crazy. Why not, if you thought you were safe? You're a long way from the rancho and a fire is a great comfort in a lonely camp.' The *segundo* spoke again to his men. 'We can find exactly where the bulls are another time. Let them have their way among the *yanqui* heifers for a few days. They have had a long walk and earned it. Better than driving them back so soon. The get and their mothers will belong to Don Felipe in time anyway. But the *patrón* will be displeased if we return without running this one out and making sure he doesn't come back a second time.'

Stanton knew what was coming next. And he knew it would be as foolish to try to reach the guns in the shelter against these odds as it would be to try to persuade the Rancho Mora crewmen that he could not be a trespasser on his own land and had the legal documents to prove it. Besides, he could not afford open conflict with Peralta, whatever their

152

differences might be. If the old don was a neighbor, then he must somehow become a friend if the Corona was to prosper. But he could not abide the hands of others upon him.

When the *vaqueros* rushed him at the *segundo's* signal, Stanton dropped the first with a short jab that smashed the man's nose. The *vaquero* rocked on the ground on his hands and knees, blowing blood and Spanish curses. He rammed a knee into the crotch of the second, but the man was no bull or he missed his mark, for he took a paralyzing, breath-venting head-butt under the ribs that drove him back over the man on the ground. He went down on his back and they were all upon him. He used his feet while he could, and his knees again, and for an instant one arm was free for a hard swing that hit home somewhere, drawing a deep grunt of hurt. Then they had him helplessly spreadeagled.

Swiftly and efficiently they tied his hands and ankles behind him with his picket rope and drew them all up together with quick, hard, angry knots. At Abelardo's order they found his packhorses out on the grass and brought them in. They retied the open pack and loaded both on the horses. Abelardo searched the shelter and seemed satisfied. He returned to where Stanton lay helpless on the ground.

'I would kill you,' he said. 'Thank Don Felipe that we haven't. He's an old man and grows soft. But I know his feelings. In a few hours you will free yourself. You have your horse, your blankets, and your guns. As soon as it is light, go. We will be back to look to your cattle in a few days. When you are out of New Mexico, write to the *patrón*. If he thinks they are of worth, he will send money for them. Stay or return and you will be shot on sight. Make no mistake about that.'

*    *    *

The fire was down to embers by the time Stanton worked out of his bonds. His first impulse was to saddle at once and pursue the Mexicans, or at least protest to Peralta, but he thought better of it. Abelardo's warning had been blunt. He would do his best to keep his promise if Stanton showed up again. So would his men.

Instead Stanton stripped, shook the dust from his clothes, and hung them in the shelter. He waded in to the creek to wash away the grime of his struggle and to cool his anger. Returning, he piled into his blankets for warmth after the chill of the creek and went to sleep almost immediately.

He was awakened by the touch of a reaching hand in the darkness. He instinctively caught the wrist and twisted the figure leaning above him off balance. It tried to turn and fell onto him with a little gasp of surprise and hurt. Instant recognition came. 'Mana. The girl he

154

so reasonlessly expected had come after all.

'It's all right,' she said quickly, struggling to regain her feet. 'It's only me. They didn't harm you—you are all right?'

He released his grip, put his arm about her, pulled her tight against him, and kissed her for an answer. Surprised, she still continued to struggle. He found her breast through the soft buckskin of her Indian dress and cupped it possessively. The nipple hardened and thrust against the leather beneath his hand. Her lips softened. Her mouth opened beneath his. Her hand touched him again and instinctively tightened as it discovered his naked back. He drank her hungrily and her tongue responded. He did not remember it had ever been like this and knew it never had been. His hand slid down her back, caressingly over her buttocks, and found the lifted hem of her dress. The satin flesh of her thigh quivered when he touched it and she lifted her head.

'No,' she breathed. 'Please.'

He kissed her again. Again she pulled away, gently trying to free herself. The dress pulled higher with the effort.

'Please,' she whispered. 'Listen to me for a minute. This wasn't the way I wanted it to be when you came back.'

'I like it fine,' Stanton said, nuzzling.

She laughed softly.

'I mean Abelardo and his men.'

'The hell with them.'

He found her lips and time stopped. When it became unbearable he tugged again impatiently at the hem of the leather dress. She thrust his hand away so sharply that he could feel the strength of her body. Contritely he freed her. She sat up beside him but made no effort to recover her bared legs.

'It mustn't be like this. Animals in rut.'

'It isn't—'

Suddenly, involuntarily, honestly, Stanton found himself saying it. Wanting to say it. The one thing he had vowed he would never say again. Not to any woman. Not under any circumstances. As long as he lived.

'I don't ask you to believe me. I can't, I suppose. But it's true. You see, I love you, 'Mana.'

She found his hand and cupped it between her own.

'We speak of love, too. But not so easily. Only in time. Long enough to know. To be sure.'

'I am,' Stanton said. 'I think I have been since I first opened my eyes and saw you.'

'But you came back to your cattle.'

'No,' Stanton corrected honestly. 'To the land. This land. Here. It's hard to explain. Maybe I don't understand, myself. I had land, once. Good land. But not like this. You're a part of that, 'Mana. I think that's what it is. To me you are this country. The living land. Through you I can speak to it, possess it, make love to it. Can you understand?'

'Yes,' 'Mana answered. 'I love this land, too. It's my home.'

'Then love me. Let me be a part of it.'

She was silent. He tightened his grip on her hand.

'You slept with me before. I dreamed it.'

'It wasn't a dream,' she said quietly. 'When you were hurt and had the fever. You chilled in the night and we had few blankets. I had to keep you warm. Yes, I slept with you many times. To save your life.'

'Save it now.'

'The other woman. You spoke of her in your fever, but I couldn't understand. You loved her?'

'She was my wife.'

'That is ended?'

'She gave my bed to another.'

'Now you want to do the same by giving your bed to me.'

Stanton flinched under the probe of her feminine logic. It was true that he had come near to bedding every woman he could find, each as a thrust at Belle for what she had so dispassionately planned and brought about. That had passed, but the challenge was just enough. For the first time he was acutely conscious of the difference in age between this barelegged girl beside him and himself. Fifteen years, he supposed. In some ways an insurmountable gap. A man could not turn

157

back time.

'No,' he said. 'To make a new beginning.'

He did not think it was explainable beyond that. For a long moment she sat motionless and silent, looking down at him. Then—easily, gracefully, unself-consciously—she lifted the pulled-up hem of her dress and peeled the garment, inside-out, over her head, revealing the full splendor of her body. He opened his blankets to her and she came to him.

'I have waited a long time,' she breathed softly in his ear.

It was true, he thought; she was saving his life again. Giving it purpose and meaning and importance. He was no longer alone.

A brief few days ago he had ridden away from the portico of the *Palacio de los Gobernadores* in Santa Fe with the documentation of an empire in an oilskin packet. Here, in an Indian bed in a brush shelter on the high grass of that domain, Spencer Stanton made love and founded a dynasty.

Later, when the night was old and a deep peace and content had come to them both, Stanton and 'Mana rose and built up the fire, carried their blankets to it, and sat in their nakedness in the warmth of its glow. For a long time there were no words and no need for any. Suddenly 'Mana laughed. It was a deep inside sound, singing with irrepressible high spirits and teasing humor.

'What is it the sisters at the convent would say? You have taken advantage of me.'

'Like hell,' Stanton said.

He kissed her, carrying her down onto her back in his arms. He touched her and her nipples hardened eagerly again, her soft brown breasts firm, red-tipped cones against the fire. He kissed them both.

'But you did,' 'Mana insisted.

He freed her and she sat up.

'It's true. You took advantage of me. I wanted to do something to make it up to you because I felt guilty.'

'About what?' he asked lazily. 'The way you make love?'

'Should I?'

'Good God, no!' Stanton said with unintentional fervency.

She laughed again.

'That's better. No. About Abelardo.'

Stanton realized she was trying to tell him something and sat up beside her with rekindled interest.

'What about Abelardo? Do you know anything about those two Mora bulls they were looking for?'

'That's what I mean. All of those poor, hungry cows of yours, after all of this long time. A man doesn't think about such things unless he's in heat himself. I went to Chato. We talked about it. There seemed no harm in borrowing one or two of Don Felipe's good breeders for a little while. But Abelardo is too conscientious since he was made *segundo*. He missed them sooner than we expected.'

'You didn't!'

'Mana nodded impishly. 'To borrow is not to steal. I'm sure that's in the *padres'* Big Book somewhere.'

'That's a distinction Abelardo and Peralta aren't going to make very easily, I think,' Stanton said wryly. 'Then those damned bulls are with my stock.'

'Up a little canyon a few miles. We moved them there to keep them closer together. Chato's with them now.'

'Mana leaned earnestly forward, putting her hand on Stanton's knee.

'When I saw the smoke of your fire, I hoped it was you and I started down here as fast as I could. But Abelardo was already coming up from the south and I was afraid that if he saw me he'd know where to look for the cattle, so I hid until dark. Later I couldn't come into your fire until they passed me and I knew they were gone.'

'You know that's what that smoke was for. And the big fire after dark. For you.'

'I know. If I could have warned you they were coming, I would have. But you knew nothing about the borrowed bulls or even where your own cattle were, so I thought Abelardo and his men couldn't make you any trouble over them. But when they came back they had your horses and packs and I was afraid they might have harmed you. Now do you see why I felt guilty?'

'And why you let me'—he paused a significant moment—'take advantage of you.'

She nodded slowly, the picture of contrition, but her eyes were dancing mischievously.

'No other reason?' he prompted.

She tried to retain her grave look as she shook her head, but laughter came instead. She surged to her knees and flung her arms about him, her mouth seeking his and her body straining against him. He lost his balance before her insistency and fell onto his back with 'Mana atop him, loving him as urgently as he had her.


## CHAPTER TWELVE

Chato was pleased with Stanton's return, but he was hotly indignant at the seizure of the *yanqui*'s packhorses and equipment by the crew from Rancho Mora. He thought he could find a few young friends among the Ute camps who were already men enough to go with him and repair the loss with no great difficulty. Stanton assured him he believed this was so and was grateful, but he was afraid a great deal of trouble and further bad feelings would result if any attempt was made to recover the seized outfit without returning the borrowed bulls.

This effectively checked the young Ute's impatience. He was quite vain about the breeding program 'Mana and he had put into operation at the temporary expense of Don Felipe Peralta and he did not want it interrupted too soon. He pointed out the Mora bulls in Stanton's herd, which looked more numerous in the confines of the little canyon than it had on the open grass where Stanton had last seen it.

'Every day it has been the same,' Chato boasted to Stanton. 'In the morning those *toros* made echoes everywhere with their bellowing. By nightfall they can only grunt a little. But you don't have to show them what to do. I'll tell you that.'

The cattle seemed content with the arrangement as well. Stanton was surprised to see how rapidly they were recovering from the rigors of the long, arid drive out the Trail. Most were starting to put on weight, taking to the country as he had himself. It was a curious feeling to look at these displaced remnants, actually so few in number, and to see them multiply in the mind's eye into an indestructible, self-perpetuating source of security, wealth, and power. To know that it was not merely fanciful dreaming, that time and determination could accomplish just that and that he now owned the means, made seaboard Virginia a faraway time and place indeed.

Stanton saw that 'Mana had her share of satisfaction, too. She pointed out that Peralta's hardier, longer-legged, shorter-backed local range line, represented by the borrowed bulls, should couple with his own normally heavier, meatier stateside stock to drop at least some calves in each generation with the best attributes of each. In time, with proper selection, an entirely new breed could emerge, well suited to the land and the long drive to market. *Yanqui* cattle, she laughingly called them. Stanton buffalo. He was amazed at her interest in the animals and amused by her proprietary attitude toward them.

He knew that before the Mora crew returned on their own he would have to make some effort to return the bulls, get back his outfit, and mend his fences as best he could with Peralta and his *segundo*—but for the moment he agreed with 'Mana and Chato. Since the bulls were here, let them earn their feed. A few more days would make little difference. And he could see no reason for keeping further watch over them. There was no sign of predators and they were prospering.

Later, when the heat of the dog days came to these lower altitudes, Stanton thought he would like to move the herd higher into the mountains to the rich meadows he had seen there. He thought they could graze to benefit up there for a few weeks while this lower grass cured out to winter feed. He had never heard of such a practice, but never had he seen country like this, either. It seemed likely it would work out well here.

When 'Mana and Stanton returned to the brush shelter, Chato accompanied them. If the young Ute noted anything new in their relationship, he made no comment. Even when 'Mana asked him to go to her *rancheria* for her belongings. Stanton had not known until that moment whether she would move permanently into the camp with him or not. He had feared her church schooling might ban that, at least until they could find a priest. But he should have known better. She was not someone who did things by halves or questioned her own decisions.

He proposed they go after her things together, supposing that some kind of a confrontation and an explanation to her people would eventually be necessary and might as well be faced now as later. Besides, he had a strong interest in how and where this girl had been born and raised and the kind of parents who could procreate such startling beauty and keen intelligence.

However, both 'Mana and Chato agreed it was not necessary or even advisable.

'Among my people,' Chato explained, 'when she is of that age, a woman can take her bed to another place. It is her right. She does not bring a man to her place. She goes to his. And she

164

does not come back.'

After Chato left Stanton cut wood and then went down along the creek with Jaime's Spanish pistol. He had not yet told 'Mana about the boy, but Jaime was one of the reasons he had been willing to defer riding to Mora for a few days. He was due in shortly and Stanton wanted to be here when he arrived, or to go in search if he became unreasonably overdue.

There was another thing, too. He realized he had come to depend upon the Missouri youngster in the brief time they were together. Royer and Luis Montoya were out there on the grass, somewhere between here and Santa Fe. Two pairs of eyes and ears were better than one. And it would be good to have another hand beside him when he rode to Mora. Even one so young.

Finding a pool along the creek to his liking, with a large rock only shallowly submerged, Stanton held the pistol close to the surface and fired both charges into the water and against the rock. Several fat trout, air bladders ruptured by the concussion, rolled belly-up and floated to the surface. He cleaned them, lined the cavities with sweet grass, and returned to camp. 'Mana was delighted, fascinated that fish could be taken in this way.

She put the fish aside in the shade against the supper hour, and Stanton helped her gather a fresh mattress of grass for their bed. The sun

165

was low when Chato returned. He bore no message from her people for 'Mana. Only her shoulder-strapped possibles bag, the little iron cooking pot he remembered, a few other utensils, and a fold of Indian blankets containing some simple articles of clothing. Stanton saw she came to him as poor in personal possessions as he was himself. It would not always be so.

Chato showed him how to cut and weave a few more stalks of brush into the side-screens of the shelter to better break the night wind, should it blow, but he refused to stay and eat. He had been away too long from his own camp, he said. 'Mana laughed at him when he was gone.

'The fish,' she said. 'Some Utes won't even catch them. Women's food, they say. They think it takes the strength from their manly parts to eat fish. The older they get, the surer they are about it. Chato's young. He worries about such things, too. He's seen a few women-men, making love to each other, giggling and doing women's work. He thinks that's what makes them that way.'

Stanton took the trout and strung them on a willow wand. He dangled it before her.

'Maybe you're worried about it, too,' he suggested.

'Yesterday, maybe,' she laughed. 'Today, no. Not after last night. I think maybe pretty soon I'll have to feed you a lot of fish if I'm to get any sleep.'

Stanton lit the fire and hung the trout over it. Presently they had their wedding supper alone, as was proper. Behind them the shelter beckoned invitingly, her possessions hanging from the corner poles. Such was a woman's touch, even in such a spartan camp.

\*       \*       \*

At midmorning of the fifth day a distant horseman appeared in the east, following the general drainage of the Cimarron and angling in such a way as to pass considerably to the north of the camp. The rider was moving unhurriedly, as though accustomed to long travel and not overusing his horse. He was holding pretty much to high ground, often skylining himself, contrary to prudent practice in Indian country. It therefore seemed likely he was keeping to high country in search of something below, or was deliberately exposing himself to attract the attention of others.

Stanton at length concluded the horseman had to be Jaime. Exposing the coals of the breakfast fire with the toe of his boot, he threw on a little wood and some green grass. 'Mana, watching from the shelter, brought out her tightly woven saddle blanket and showed him how to swing it over the fire in a horizontal whirling motion that caused a turbulence in the rising heat. This broke the thin thread of dense white smoke into a series of explosive little puff-balls that rose into the air like punctuation marks against the sky.

Almost at once the rider changed direction and rode directly toward them. In an hour he was recognizable beyond mistake and a little before noon Jaime rode into the camp. 'Mana studied him as he approached and Stanton saw approval in her eyes. Knowing Stanton would want to talk to the boy, she took his horse. Jaime's eyes followed her appreciatively.

'I should have known there was something more than some damned old cattle up here,' he told Stanton by way of greeting.

'Mana came back and Stanton introduced them. Jaime's Spanish was not adequate for a full understanding of the relationship, but his expression and manner made his admiration clear. Being a woman 'Mana found this sufficient. Jaime had a haunch of antelope from a two-day-old kill in the *mochila* Armijo had given them in Albuquerque. 'Mana took this welcome addition to their scant supplies and began to prepare it for the fire. Stanton and Jaime sat down in the shade of the shelter.

The boy had seen nothing of Royer or Luis Montoya. There had been no traffic behind him on the Santa Fe Trail, which he had closely paralleled most of his route. In fact the opposite had been true and he was disturbed about it.

'Something's up,' he said earnestly. 'You

know how news travels out here. Or, rather, you don't. Nobody. Just that it does. Like the wind. Look how they knew we were coming three or four days before we got the wagons and your stock to the Canadian crossing. It was the same when the train finally got into Santa Fe. And don't tell me General Armijo wasn't all primed for us when we turned up with that jack-string in Albuquerque.'

Stanton nodded at the phenomenon of communication about which Jaime complained.

'Once I'd topped Glorieta Pass and started down the other side, like you told me,' Jaime continued, 'I had to keep pulling off out of sight and letting others going up pass. Seemed like everybody was heading for Santa Fe. And they had everything with them that'd shoot.'

'No idea what's afoot?'

Jaime shook his head.

'And no way to find out. Don't know enough of the lingo yet. But it must be something important. That's hard country. Those are hill people. Like mine. I know them, even if they are Mexican and Indian. They wouldn't leave their places at this season, crops in and needing tending, unless it was for something as important as hell. I'm glad we're clear up here where it can't affect us.'

'From here on, son,' Stanton said quietly, 'anything that happens in New Mexico affects us. We're part of it now.'

He told Jaime about the ambush reception waiting for him in the *cantina* on the *Camino Real*, the acquisition of title to the Corona, the session with Royer and Montoya in the La Fonda tavern, and his private transaction with Sol Wetzel. He did this quietly when 'Mana's attention was elsewhere. Not that he wished to withhold anything from her. Rather, he wanted to wait for the most opportune moment possible, so that his revelation of ownership would have the greatest possible effect and would please her the most.

'Mana's smoke signals brought another rider in presently. Chato came up along the creek, singing in a high, chanting voice.

'What was all that?' Stanton asked him as he dismounted.

'Mana answered for the young Ute.

'A war song,' she said with a smile.

'I thought when I saw your smoke, "Good!"' Chato said, ' "Today the *yanqui* rides with the *toros* to Mora. Maybe Abelardo will make a little fight with us about that. So I will sing a song and be ready." '

'Just in case, huh?'

'One can hope. Just a little fight.'

Stanton laughed.

'We'll see, *amigo*.'

He introduced Jaime to the Ute. They were of the same age and size and strangely not as alien as Stanton would have supposed. They sized each other up with the wariness of strange animals, but seemingly found nothing to disapprove or challenge. Jaime offered his hand. Chato took it gravely. Thus, wordlessly, they reached some kind of accord of their own.

The good smell of red meat smoked over embers by its own burning juices came from the fire and 'Mana called them to eat. This time, his manhood safe, Chato did not refuse the food. He sat beside Jaime, eating appreciatively without utensils but with an Indian's uncanny ability to avoid burned fingers and drippings upon his person in a delicate way that was civilized by any standard.

'Jaime thinks something important is going on in Santa Fe,' Stanton told 'Mana and Chato when they were finished. 'We don't know what it is. But we do know we have to return Don Felipe's bulls, get back the outfit and pack-horses his men took here, and make some kind of a peace with him, if we can. Both of you can be helpful in that. They may have word of what's going on in Santa Fe at Mora. And maybe the priest will be there on his rounds. At least we can find where he is. I'm not taking any chances on this woman changing her mind.'

'Mana laughed. The two boys moved off to saddle the horses. 'Mana looked after them.

'*Qué hombre, yanqui!*' she said in mocking marvel. 'Look. I have not yet passed my first blood and already two sons!'

# CHAPTER THIRTEEN

They moved the cattle out of the little canyon where they had been hidden onto the open grass again. The animals spread out contentedly along the water to graze, as though at home. Often difficult to drive and impossible to lead, the two young Mora bulls were as docile as fresh barn cows, plodding along with their underparts swaying like swollen udders.

When keeping the bulls moving allowed, Jaime and Chato rode together, each using the unintelligible words of his own tongue, but with tones and gestures and poses so expressive that they were able to maintain a lively conversation, much punctuated by laughter at common misconceptions and mutual enjoyment. Their horses tired quickly because of frequent challenges and the high animal spirits of their riders.

Stanton had returned the Spanish pistol. Jaime would not surrender the Henry rifle Stanton had entrusted to his care, but he passed Chato the holster belt and showed him how to use the weapon General Armijo had given to him. The young Ute was fascinated by the pistol and vain of its temporary possession. But when they flushed a flock of wild turkeys in a pinon grove near sunset, he brought down his bird with a trade-tipped arrow from his short saddle-bow.

They camped at the mouth of a canyon where another Indian trail came down from the mountains. 'Mana said that it led to Taos, which really wasn't a town at all but a series of Mexican villages and two very old, still occupied Indian pueblos on a bench high above the head of the Rio Grande canyon. Chato had no use for the Taoseños, Mexican or Indian. They were malcontents and plotters. All trouble started with them, but others usually had to pay.

He showed Jaime that there had been recent traffic down the Taos trail. The hoofprints of a pair of horses were quite plain in places. However, to Stanton's amusement, Jaime noted that one of the animals was shod, and the shape of the shoe looked more like a Missouri mule to him.

At noon the next day the high saddle and naked twin peaks of El Cumbre were in view. Both Chato and 'Mana were as incredulous as Peralta's *segundo* that Stanton had crossed that pass with his packhorses on the way back from Santa Fe. But they believed him and eyed him with new respect.

'Mana and Chato wanted to leave the Mora bulls on the pasturage where they had found them. Stanton wanted to make a proper arrival at Peralta's place, and he thought the bulls were necessary for that. The old *hacendado* would be crusty at best, and for generations he

173

and his line had been accustomed to a high hand as far as their own affairs and possessions were concerned. But Stanton knew Peralta was of what Virginians called the old school. He would react most favorably to an honest and straightforward explanation of facts and an offer of suitable amends.

'Mana and Jaime were inclined to agree, but Chato was full of dark forebodings.

'Maybe,' he snorted. 'If you can get to the *patrón*. I don't know about gentlemen. But you are *yanqui*. You don't know that Abelardo. He is a fierce one. He promised that he'll kill you if he sees you again. That's what he'll try to do. So will his *vaqueros*. They fear him. Everybody does. "Don Felipe's *lobo*," they call him. "The Peralta wolf."'

'But back at camp you were hoping for a fight with him,' Stanton pointed out mildly.

'That is different,' Chato replied haughtily, as though the explanation was self-evident and incontestable. 'I am a Ute.'

Stanton laughed at the assurance with which the boy stated the vanity, but he was fully aware of the validity of Chato's sober warning. And although she said nothing, he saw that 'Mana was equally concerned. Only Jaime, when he understood what the exchange had been, was unconcerned.

'Varmint like that,' he said, 'only thing to do's go right in and fix his wagon. Get done what's got to be done. A wolf can get hisself

174

killed as easy as any other critter, if he's trapped right.'

They discussed it further at night camp. 'Mana came up with the most practical solution.

'I'm known there,' she said. 'Don Felipe has been kind to me since I was a little girl. His *favorita*, he used to call me. They won't know I had anything to do with the bulls until I tell them. Don Felipe will listen to me, and he'll believe what I say. He'll give orders to Abelardo. Then it will be safe for you to bring the bulls in.'

So it was agreed.

In midmorning they pulled up in a stand of timber at the point of closest practical approach to the Peralta headquarters. The buildings themselves were obscured by a low knoll on the floor of the valley where they lay. But the smell of kitchen fires was in the air and dogs about the place could be plainly heard. 'Mana left them at the edge of the timber and rode out across the grass, disappearing in a few minutes over the crest of the knoll.

Stanton grew uneasy with her out of view. He wanted to see her approach, be certain of her reception. Ordering the boys to remain where they were, he rode rapidly after 'Mana. A few yards from the top of the knoll he dismounted, ground-tied his horse, and ran the remaining distance, flinging himself down in the grass and wriggling forward to where he could see.

Riding easily and unhurriedly, 'Mana was almost into the compound, heading toward the broad *ramada* across the front of the main house. Aside from a couple of dogs trotting out toward her and barking inquisitively, there was no movement in the ranch yard.

The corral, which Stanton thought should be empty of stock at this hour of the day, still contained half a dozen unsaddled working ponies. They were milling nervously. Back of a long, low building, possibly a storeroom or granary which was attached to the commissary where he had made his purchases on his previous visit, several saddled horses were tied to a rail. He could not tell how many.

'Mana tied her horse to the rail in front of the main house and stepped under the *ramada*. She paused momentarily, as though curious that no one had come out to meet her, then went on across to the door. It was suddenly jerked open from within. 'Mana wheeled in alarm and darted back toward her horse. Two men leaped out through the door after her.

At once guns across the compound opened up on them. The firing seemed to come from two positions. One was the side windows of the commissary. The other was behind a debris heap at the lower end of the yard. He thought two men were in the commissary. He could not tell how many were behind the pile of junk.

Heavy return fire on both positions opened

up from the front of the house. The two men under the *ramada* seized 'Mana at the rail before she could free her horse. They dragged her roughly back to the door and thrust her inside. Stanton had no difficulty recognizing one as the arrogant, powerful figure of Bennett Royer, still dressed in the outfit he had appropriated from Stanton's trunk. The door closed behind them and the firing across the yard halted for want of targets.

Stanton rolled back and sat up to signal Jaime and Chato forward, but the sound of gunfire had been enough for them. They were already out onto the grass, racing recklessly toward him. He returned his attention to the scene below, suddenly as peaceful as it had been when 'Mana rode into it.

There was no way of knowing what had happened down there, what was happening to 'Mana now. It was enough that Royer was involved. Stanton cursed the open in which Peralta's forebears had located their cottonwood-shaded headquarters. No doubt it had originally been planned to facilitate defense. But it sure as hell made relief as difficult as attack. There was no satisfactory cover by which closer mounted approach could be made from any side.

Jaime and Chato came thundering up, flung down where he had left his own horse, and wormed forward to join Stanton. He told them what had happened and pointed out as many of the saddled horses as were visible behind the storeroom.

'I don't know how many of them there are or what they want,' he said. 'But they've got 'Mana in the house. Probably the old man, too. It looks like they've been cut off from their horses by the men in the yard. But I can't figure where the rest of Peralta's crew is. I don't think there are more than three or four of them in the yard and the store.'

Chato went scuttling through the grass along the knoll a hundred yards or so to one side. In unspoken agreement Jaime worked out an equal distance on the other. Both were back quickly. From his angle Chato could count a total of eight saddled horses racked behind the storeroom. There were no others. From his Jaime reported two men, obviously not defenders, on guard near what appeared to be a tool shed just around the near corner of the main house. Neither spotted any more Peralta men.

'Six in the house, then,' Stanton said. 'Two outside. Checkmated for the moment. But it won't stay that way. When they work up enough sand, they'll make a rush and clear the yard. There's enough of them to do it. Only way to stop them is get down there before they try.'

'Charge,' Chato said. 'That's what my uncle would do. There were only thirty of us and no guns when he attacked your whole train of wagons.'

'And we're three,' Stanton answered impatiently. 'What kind of a charge is that? We'd be shot out of our saddles before we hit any kind of cover at all. Worse, they could count us and know exactly what they're up against. If we can't override them we'll have to worry the living hell out of them.'

'We can make it through the grass,' Jaime said. 'Belly-button it.'

Stanton nodded agreement.

'But not from this side. Not with those two you spotted at the corner of the house. Too easy to step around and see us. Make for that pile of junk at the other end of the yard. One of Don Felipe's men is there and it's about the best cover on that side.'

Chato unbelted the Spanish pistol and handed it to Jaime.

'My bow is best for this.'

Jaime took the weapon and passed the Henry rifle to Stanton. The boys slithered down the slope, circling through the grass as instructed. Within a few yards their swift, prone movement was almost indiscernible. Stanton knew he could not do as well. His one hope was that Royer would not expect outside interference and that his concern for the guns that pinned him down from the store and the yard would keep his attention there rather than on the approaches.

It was an interminable crawl. Heat beat

down on Stanton's back and surged up from the earth at the roots of the grass. Foxtails encasing the ripening seed-heads of the grass penetrated his clothing to prick and rasp his skin and fill his boots with irritating needles. He was restricted to awkward, crablike movement because he had to carry the rifle in one hand. Finally he thrust it down his back, through the collar of his shirt, and under his belt and so made better time without exposing himself so much. Even then he lost track of the boys for rods at a time and feared they might become separated. But in the end they reached the far side of the compound and moved in toward it.

As they worked closer to the junk pile Stanton had selected as target, they could see a man crouching behind it. Stanton was astonished to recognize he was a priest. He had hiked the skirt of his cassock up for freer movement and tucked it under the cord of his girdle, exposing his sandaled feet and stout, knotty, brown lower legs. He had a double Spanish pistol very similar to Jaime's gripped in one hand and was watching the main house intently. Stanton flipped a pebble toward him in warning of their presence.

The *padre* stiffened instantly and turned slowly, peering. Finally he spotted them where they lay in the last cover of yard weeds, thirty feet away. He brightened but showed the pistol with spread upturned hands and a rueful shrug in signal it was empty. Stanton eyed the strip of bare earth they must cross to reach him. His attention shifted to the windows of the store.

'I wish whoever's in there knew we were here and could make a diversion for us,' he muttered to the boys beside him.

'If it's Abelardo, maybe he'll understand,' Chato said.

He rolled over on his back to give his bow horizontal freedom. Carefully stretching his arms out above his head so that no motion showed above the weed tops, he fitted an arrow. He sighted painstakingly, upside down, and let the arrow fly. It streaked silently across the yard and imbedded itself in the crown timber supporting the opening of one of the commissary windows. Instantly cautious movement appeared within as a man examined the arrow, without touching it or otherwise exposing himself to the house, and sighted out along the shaft to determine the direction of its flight and source.

Stanton thought they must be visible from this angle, for the man quickly disappeared. A moment later a muzzle was thrust through each of the windows and each flung a shot in quick succession across the yard at the house. There was a rattle of return fire.

Stanton and the boys were in motion with the first shot, sprinting across the short bare space to the debris pile where the *padre* crouched. They reached it and flung themselves down beside the cleric without drawing a shot or apparently any attention from the house. The echoes rolled away and the compound fell silent again. The *padre* gripped Stanton's shoulder with feeling, but shrugged in answer to his unspoken query.

'*Quién sabe?*' he said softly. 'I came in from the Taos trail yesterday. It is the time for my regular *visita* here. Don Felipe ordered an early mass for this morning. It is my custom before such a mass to hold my own communion with the good God—'

He smiled and pointed out the house privy a few yards away, then gestured with the discharged pistol.

'I have a fear of snakes, so I took this with me when I left the house. They must have been waiting here before daylight. As the *vaqueros* began to awaken and come out of the bunkhouse down there to make water and wash up, they hit them over the head and dragged them off, one at a time, so there was no alarm. I couldn't get back to the house without being seen, so I had to stay where I was. Only Abelardo and one other were able to break away. I think they broke out a back window of the bunkhouse and got into the store there, where there were guns. When they started shooting from there I tried to get to them, but this is as far as I got because those *cabrones* ran across and broke into the house and started shooting back from there. Now I have no more shots.'

'We'll try to make up for that,' Stanton promised shortly. 'They have Don Felipe?'

The *padre* nodded.

'With two or three of the servants, I think. And the girl. You saw her?'

'She came with us.'

Stanton appraised the situation again and made his decision. A trade was better than greater risk. Raising his voice, he called across the compound.

'Royer, this is Spencer Stanton. I now have all of my men in place. We have you completely cut off from your horses.'

There was no response from the house. Stanton repeated the challenge in Spanish for those to whom the first had been unintelligible. There was still no response.

'We want Don Felipe and the servants and the girl, Royer,' Stanton continued. 'Send them out. When we have them you're free to go. We'll hold our fire.'

He repeated this in Spanish also so there would be no misunderstanding of the terms among any of them. The silence persisted. The *padre* stirred beside Stanton.

'It is not always easy to make sinners come forward, not even with the promise of eternal salvation, *señor*,' he said. 'Not in the face of their transgressions. I think they want Don Felipe. I'm afraid that's what they came here for. I beg you to use care. It would be a sad day

183

for this part of *Nuevo Méjico* if any harm came to him.'

'It won't,' Stanton answered grimly. 'That girl in there with him is mine.'

The *padre* showed surprise at this but said nothing. Jaime suddenly rammed his elbow into Stanton and unholstered his gun.

'Here they come!'

The door of the house jerked open. 'Mana, Don Felipe, and a frightened servant woman, so fat she trembled as she waddled, were hustled out under the *ramada*. Their hands had been tied behind their backs and a man gripped the elbows of each on either side. Royer and, as Stanton had suspected, Luis Montoya brought up the rear. Stanton realized there were now eight, so they had brought in the two who had been on watch in back of the house and this was it.

There was one other nondescript Yankee in the group. The others were Mexican or Indian. The dregs of Santa Fe. All had guns in their hands and pressed so tightly against their hostages that to fire upon them was impossible, even at this close range.

They came out from under the *ramada* as fast as they could, pushing the reluctant hostages at a half run. They headed straight across the yard toward a corner of the storeroom behind which their horses were still waiting. It was a short gauntlet from either Stanton's position or the store. Little more than a hundred feet. Once across they would be gone. Stanton raised up behind the broken, solid-wood wheel of an old *carreta* on the junk pile before him. Royer saw him and fired vindictively as he moved. The slug stung a thick splinter of the rotten wood against Stanton's face.

'Mana saw the blood come and doubled suddenly forward as though she had tripped and lost her balance. The two at her elbows tried to jerk her upright but she twisted from their grips and went on to the ground, rolling swiftly back to cut the feet from under Felipe Peralta and his double escort. They had to let the old man go to keep from falling themselves, and the fat, frightened servant tripped over her employer's body.

The men beside her could not check the fall of so much soft weight and she went down shrieking on top of the other two hostages. From beneath the squirming pile of skirts and legs 'Mana's voice rang out triumphantly.

'Now, *hombre mío! Chihuahua!*'


## CHAPTER FOURTEEN

For a moment of consternation and indecision they were all sitting ducks. Royer's men were grappling for holds with which to get the entangled hostages onto their feet again. Royer and Montoya, seeing the danger, were clawing at their men, trying to pull them away.

'Forget the goddamned women!' Royer was shouting. 'Bring the old man! Bring the old man!'

But Felipe Peralta was at the bottom of the heap, covered by the women, and a crossfire was lacing those on their feet. With the particular viciousness of his people when they killed in war, Chato put an arrow through the throat of a man aiming a kick at the fat servant on the ground. As the man fell, choking on his own blood, Stanton saw that the arrow shaft stuck out the same distance before and behind. A ball from a musket or rifle in the store struck another from behind and broke his back as he bent to tug at the women.

The other Yankee in the group managed to seize 'Mana by her breasts and leaned back furiously to prize her up bodily by them. Stanton shot him through the head with the Henry rifle.

Jaime, with remembered reasons of his own, fired the first barrel of the Spanish pistol at Bennett Royer. The ball struck the man in the side of one buttock, knocking that leg from under him. He rolled and bounded up in a dragging run for the corner of the storeroom. Emptying what charges they had left as they moved, Montoya and the three others still on their feet followed him.

Jaime tried again with his other barrel for

Royer and missed. The man made the corner of the storeroom and dove around it, escaping the angle of fire. Another shot from the store took a Mexican behind Montoya in mid-stride and the hard adobe of the yard tore his face as he pitched onto it.

Stanton held the Navy Colt in his hand, the hammer back, but the heat of anger and outrage was gone and four men already lay dead in the yard. He did not fire again. Montoya and the two remaining men rounded the corner of the storeroom at a full run and disappeared after Royer.

Abelardo, 'the Peralta wolf,' charged from the store with the *vaquero* who had been with him there. They halted when they heard the clatter of escaping horses back of the storeroom. Abelardo crossed quickly to Don Felipe and the two women, helping them to their feet and assuring himself that they were unhurt. 'Mana ran into Stanton's arms and touched the place on his cheek where the splinter from Royer's first shot had struck. Her fingers came away sticky and he realized for the first time that he was bleeding.

The *padre* came out unhurriedly from behind the junk pile and handed his spent pistol to the *vaquero* who had been in the store with Abelardo.

'It needs recharging,' he said calmly. 'I think your *compañeros* are in the meat house behind the kitchen. They dragged them off in that direction.'

The *vaquero* hurried away and the *padre* approached Stanton and 'Mana.

'This is Father Frederico,' 'Mana said with obvious affection. 'He doesn't like to admit to anything that long a time ago, but he baptized me.'

Father Frederico looked at Stanton.

'*Tu novio?*' he asked the girl bluntly. 'Your sweetheart? I understood him to make some such claim when they were holding you in there.'

'A little more than that, I think,' 'Mana answered with a smile.

'He is a *yanqui*,' the priest said in stern disapproval. 'And he is no boy.' He looked at the bodies in the yard and turned back to Stanton. 'I begged you to take care. Is that what you call this?'

Stanton smiled, wondering if the bombastic cleric realized his cassock was still kited up above his knees.

'As you say, Father,' he answered, 'it's not always easy to make sinners come forward or repent their sins.'

Father Frederico frowned, but 'Mana laughed. Abelardo and Don Felipe crossed to them. It was a difficult moment for the wolf of Mora.

'It seems that I will not have to kill you after all,' the *segundo* said stiffly.

'Good,' Stanton said. 'Your bulls are at the

188

edge of timber on the other side of that knoll.'

Still laughing, 'Mana added, 'I stole them, 'Lardo. Chato and I did. But only to borrow for a little while.'

'Steal? You? My little *inocencia?*'

Father Frederico started to draw himself up in indignation, then became aware of his still kited cassock. He shook it down and smoothed the skirt, then drew himself up again.

'What evil has come among us?'

He phrased it as a question but he was looking accusingly at Stanton.

'Oh, it's worse than you think,' 'Mana said with an impish glint in her eyes. 'Much worse. I think today you will have to marry me.'

'To this one—this *yanqui*—this old man?' the *padre* protested, raising his voice in sonorous abjuration. 'No, by my sacred order! Such haste is unseemly. It displeases man and God. Such things take time. Much time. The wisdom of many friends. The traditions of your people. There must be much searching of the soul—'

The cleric was enthusiastically building himself up to a proper professional denunciation. Smiling sweetly and utterly unconcerned, 'Mana cut him short.

'If you don't, Father, I have been in sin for more than a week already.' She shrugged. 'But then, of course, we can go before the Ute council according to custom. I suppose it's really the same thing.'

189

Father Frederico choked on his own words. Stanton could see that he was utterly dumbfounded, now that he faced a truth rather than the half-meant teasing he hoped it to be. Felipe Peralta seemed equally thunderstruck and concerned. He looked about uncomfortably.

The *vaquero* who had gone in search of his broken-headed and imprisoned fellows had returned from the rear of the house with them in tow. They were at the horse trough in the corral, gingerly bathing their split scalps and knotted heads.

'I think we had best go inside,' the old don said. 'There is much to be cleaned up out here and it will not be pleasant to watch. See to it, 'Lardo.'

The *segundo* nodded and moved off toward his battered crew. Jaime touched Stanton's elbow.

'Chato and I'll bring in our horses and the bulls,' he said. Then, under his breath so 'Mana and the others could not hear, 'But I wish I'd got that bastard with that second shot!'

Stanton gripped the boy's shoulder gratefully.

'You did just fine, son. Both of you. Thanks.'

Jaime nodded and moved down the yard with Chato toward the knoll behind which they had left the horses. Felipe Peralta led the way to the *ramada* of the main house. He paused there to allow 'Mana and Father Frederico to enter ahead of him. As Stanton approached, the don checked him momentarily.

'I do not have words now for what 'Mana just told us out there,' he said gravely. 'But there is something I want you to know. This is a very old house and you are the first *yanqui* ever to enter it. I want you to know you are welcome. Let that be a measure of my gratitude for what you and those two young men did out there this morning. Those were very dangerous men. They intended to kill me if I did not go with them.'

'But why?' Stanton asked, still baffled by Royer's and Montoya's motives.

'Treason, *señor*. For money. They boasted about it. But come, the others must hear. It's a sad and tragic business.'

Don Felipe gestured courteous invitation and Stanton passed into the house ahead of him.

Peralta's report was stark and shocking. Jaime's uneasiness over the movement of even the poorest of the hill people toward Santa Fe was justified in spades. The pressure for tax reform and relief for the *paisanos*, about which Stanton had heard rumbles from all quarters since his arrival, had exploded into open revolt.

The match that had touched off the long-primed fuse was a new edict by Governor Pérez. It ordered prohibitive additional levies on goods and merchandise of any kind moving into, out of, or through the capitol. Even the animals and crude carts of the humblest farmers, as well as professional freight outfits, were to be taxed for passage, laden, through the streets.

Stanton wondered if the arrival of a burro train of Albuquerque wool, consigned to Sol Wetzel for shipment to the States, might have baited Pérez into this rash move in retaliation against his arch enemy, General Armijo. With a certain admiration for the man's deviousness, he also wondered if the possibility of this had not prompted the general to propose the wool shipments in the first place.

Outraged and desperate country people began to converge on the capitol from all directions in protest. Pérez declared martial law. Royer and Montoya, with no love for the governor, joined a strong rebel force approaching from the north. They found it led in part by a Taos Indian, José Gonzales, a long-time dissident well known to Father Frederico. He accepted their offer to betray the governor's defenses.

Pérez met them north of the city but was driven back. The rebels entered Santa Fe in triumph. Ruffians recruited by Royer and Montoya succeeded in opening the *palacio* to them. The governor was forced to flee for his life. A mob overtook him on the Agua Fria road, within two miles of the plaza, and he was cut to pieces. His head was returned to the *palacio* on an Indian lance.

While the excitement was at its peak, before other approaching groups could enter the city and help stabilize the mob, the *Taoseño*, José Gonzales, was proclaimed the new governor and Pérez's hated edicts were struck down. To all intents and purposes, law and legal government ceased to exist in the province.

'You ask why they sent here for me,' Don Felipe said sadly. 'Those angry, wild, foolish men! The best of them are but poor corn farmers, drunk on blood and *aguardiente*. They can't make a government and they know it—or will when they have a chance to sober up and see what they've done.

'But they found gold in the treasury. Mine is an old family. An important one for many years, with influence in Mexico City. So they offer ten thousand *yanqui* dollars for my head, dead or alive. The same for other men of importance, too, I suppose. Alive, to support this wretched Indian and urge Mexico City to confirm him as governor. An impossible thing. Dead, if we refuse, so we can't work against him. It makes no difference to ruffians like this Royer and Luis Montoya, so long as they collect the head money.'

'The longer the mob holds the city, the harder it'll be to break up,' Stanton said. 'What do you plan, Don Felipe? Get word to other *hacendados*, pool your forces, and attempt a counterrevolt?'

'It's already too late for that,' Peralta answered heavily. 'And none of us is a military man. Too many would die.'

'What about Manuel Armijo?'

'I have nothing personal against him, but he is known to be ambitious. Too ambitious to be trusted.'

'Trusted with what?' Stanton asked. 'At least Santa Fe's at stake, if not the whole province. What's so wrong with ambition? If you promised to make him governor, what ambition would the general have after that? The people of the lower valley are solidly behind him. I saw that. They believe he's for them. I think he could raise as big an army as he needed.'

Don Felipe looked thoughtful. Father Frederico put his hand on the old man's knee.

'I know this Indian, Don Felipe,' he said. 'This Gonzales. He's a braggart. A man of no courage, no honor. I think he would run from a strong enough show of force.'

'It's dangerous to cut loose the dogs of war,' Peralta protested.

'Any more dangerous than to have the government in the hands of a mob?' Stanton countered. 'Look what happened in your own yard this morning. Do you want the same thing happening on other ranchos and farms, on the streets of your towns, in private houses, wherever they think there's something they

194

want? One time I didn't fight back. After that I swore I'd never turn my cheek again. And I won't. If you think you can persuade your influential people to accept General Armijo, to back him for governor if he clears the city, I'll try to get him to march on Santa Fe at once.'

'No,' the old don said. 'I can't permit that. You've done enough already. We must mend our own fences. You are *yanqui*. That is dangerous enough. With even the little people up in arms, it is impossible. If a message is to be sent to Manuel Armijo, I will take it myself.'

'Nonsense,' Stanton protested with conviction. 'You're too well known, too valuable for getting others to back the plan. Besides the rebels need you too much. You'd be playing right into their hands, if they're keeping any kind of watch at all. But they won't be paying attention to any Yankees right now. They're too full of their own affairs. I will get through a lot more easily. And Armijo will listen to me. I know how to make sure he does.'

Don Felipe rose, shaking his head stubbornly.

'We won't discuss it further,' he said firmly. 'I must make up my mind about General Armijo. It's a difficult decision. But we have other matters requiring attention here. If you will excuse us, I wish a few words with 'Mana and Father Frederico.'

Stanton looked at 'Mana. She nodded reassuringly. He rose and picked up his hat.

'Of course,' he said agreeably. 'I'll be outside.'

He stepped out into the sun of the yard. Chato and Jaime had returned with the horses and the two Mora bulls. They were watering them down by the corral. The door of the storeroom had been opened and Stanton's packhorses brought up. Abelardo and a *vaquero* were saddling them with the packed outfit that had been confiscated at his camp.

The yard was again at peace, as though violence was far distant in time as well as place. There was quiet and the noonday heat was pleasant. It was hard to realize that beyond the mountains towering over Mora there was tumult in Santa Fe and soon other men must die.

In a few minutes 'Mana appeared on the *ramada* behind him.

'Bring Chato and Jaime,' she called.

He whistled up the boys and reentered the house with them.

Father Frederico was alone in the room. He had donned a surplice over his cassock and had an open prayer book in his hand.

'You will stand here,' he said to Stanton, indicating a place before him.

An inner door opened and 'Mana appeared on the arm of Don Felipe Peralta. She was beaming radiantly as they crossed the room to Stanton.

'Understand,' the old man said, 'I do not

196

approve. But I must give my blessing, and I do.'

He stepped back to stand with Jaime and Chato, and Father Frederico began to read.

'Dearly beloved—' he intoned.

In the quiet dignity of this old room, attended by a Ute Indian, a boy from the Missouri hills, and an aging descendant of the grandees of Old Spain, Spencer Stanton was married to the golden girl who had nursed him back to health and shared his bed on this New Mexican grass.

He smiled, thinking of her excitement when the time came to tell her of the documents in the oilskin packet and what else she had acquired besides a husband.

When the priest finished his benediction and closed the book, Stanton kissed her. Afterward 'Mana clung to him.

'Don Felipe has made up his mind,' she said. 'He agrees with you and Father Frederico. General Armijo is the best hope of restoring order in Santa Fe. You still intend to go to Albuquerque?'

Stanton nodded.

'Even if I forbid it on my wedding day?'

Stanton nodded again.

'See what I told you, Father?' she complained to the *padre*, making a little face. 'Already I can do nothing with him.'

She turned back to Stanton, putting her arms about his neck.

'We will have many years together,' she said. 'Many times you will have to do this. I know that. It's best for me to learn how to let you go now. Come, *yanqui*. I'll help you make up your saddle-roll.'

## CHAPTER FIFTEEN

From the gaunt, harsh saddle of El Cumbre Pass Stanton looked back down onto the high grass. All was well there. Couriers were on their way to other landowners Peralta respected and trusted. Abelardo had stationed sentries on approaches from the south. The rest of the crew had been pulled in to duties close to the Mora *hacienda*. Gaps in the compound had been closed for better defense, if it should become necessary.

Stanton doubted that another attempt would be made to seize Don Felipe, now that the element of surprise was lacking. But the prize offered made anything possible and Abelardo's precautions seemed wise. Father Frederico had agreed to stay on for a time. He would see that Don Felipe remained where he was until the course of events at Santa Fe was determined.

Stanton would have preferred that 'Mana remain at Mora as well. But she was as insistent in her own way as he was in his. She was determined to return to the Corona and await his homecoming there. He could not dissuade her. Escorted by Jaime and Chato, she had ridden north with the outfit Abelardo had returned to him.

She would have much to do, she claimed. Looking after the stock. Improving their camp with the new outfit. Getting it ready for his return. He was certain there would be no rebel incursion that far north. At least at this point. So he had humored her.

As he kicked up his horse and rode down through the great boulder field above timberline on the western slope of El Cumbre, Stanton thought of what lay ahead on this side of the mountains. He had no doubt that with assurances of the support of Felipe Peralta and such other influential *hacendados* as the old don's messengers could reach, Manuel Armijo would move at once to oppose the rebels now in control of the capitol.

The general was too shrewd a businessman and politician not to seize such a guaranteed opportunity to become the savior of the province. What the cost might be in time, men, money, and concessions was anybody's guess. Armijo would drive a hard bargain. That much was sure.

As Stanton's own country had learned recently enough, the price of liberty and just government came high. Whether the cost was bearable was to be decided by those who knew the local situation and history better than any foreigner possibly could.

It was not the eventual solution of the problems in Santa Fe that concerned Stanton most at this point. It was a rule of human experience that the rights of the people, with competent leadership, would be served in time. The old adobe city had been weathering despots and uprisings and bloody revolt for more than two hundred years. It would survive.

He was thinking of what he must do himself. The real reason he had insisted upon making this ride. He had made a personal tactical mistake. One he had repeated more than once since entering New Mexico. He thought he was about out of chances to rectify it.

He had underestimated the enemy. He had let Bennett Royer challenge him and had not called him on it in the dry morning camp of the wagons. He had let Brock and Hagen lag behind him when Chato was leading them after his uncle's raiders to recover their stolen horses. He had only defended his life and taken no other toll in the little *cantina* on the *Camino Real*. And he had demanded only what was his from Royer and Luis Montoya in the La Fonda tavern.

So Brock was dead. Hagen yet lived, the last he knew. So did Royer and Montoya. Instead of slinking out of Santa Fe, banished and disgraced, they had evened their sullen score with Albino Pérez and had the former governor's bloody head to prove it.

They had ridden back into the city as avenging conquerors, champions of the people. Now they were on the good side of the self-declared new governor, Gonzales. Unquestionably they had behind them the full force of whatever power the *Taoseño* had been able to seize. Their bold attempt to kidnap Don Felipe Peralta left no doubt of that.

And at Mora Stanton had let another brief moment of advantage slip past, trading it for the safety of 'Mana and the old don and his fat serving woman. Now time was running out. Governor Pérez records would not remain secret for long. Soon the fact of a *yanqui's* acquisition of the Corona Grant would become common knowledge. Royer and Montoya would learn what he had paid for it. That in itself would make it in their eyes a stake worth gambling for.

This time they could bring the fight to him. On their own terms and with the sanction of the government, so long as their rebel friends occupied the *Palacio de los Gobernadores*. It was for Manuel Armijo to save New Mexico. It was to save the Corona that Spencer Stanton was again crossing these mountains. It could be done by killing two men. A third if he was alive.

*     *     *

Manuel Armijo was not at his modest *finca* on the banks of the lower Rio Grande. Stanton found him in his impressive family mansion off of the Albuquerque plaza. He was in the uniform of the Army of the Republic of Mexico. A tense air of business stirring was about him and he seemed much more preoccupied than before.

'A sorry business in Santa Fe,' he agreed when Stanton told him of the support he brought from the north. 'A legal government must be established as soon as possible, of course. But I am surprised the *ricos* up there would select you as emissary. Old Don Felipe, in particular. A *yanqui*. Most unusual.'

'I was able to be of service to him in another matter.'

Armijo gave him a sharp, searching look, but did not press for details, as though they were of little moment.

'One must suppose so. A valuable one, at that. You and I must have an understanding in this regard. I am not Felipe Peralta.'

'I'm not likely to make the mistake of supposing that, General.'

'Good. I intend to retake Santa Fe. In the best interests of the rebels as well as the province. My plans are complete. I am determined to become the next legal governor. I regard it as my patriotic duty. I am the only one qualified.'

'Or strong enough,' Stanton suggested.

'That, too,' Armijo agreed without a trace of self-consciousness, 'although that can't be determined until the fighting is over. The message you bring makes success much more certain. The *ricos* have always had great influence over the *paisanos*. It is a fact of life here that they control their thinking from the day they're born. And there's nothing to be gained by killing farmers who belong in their fields. Much of that may now be avoided, thanks to you.'

'You have your duty; I have mine.'

'Precisely. You make my point. What I meant when I warned I was not Felipe Peralta. I'm grateful to you but I don't accept obligation. To anyone. To a *yanqui*, a foreigner, most of all. There will be no rewards, no special concessions. My responsibility is to my people, my country. I have no friends. I can't afford to if I am to become governor.'

Stanton thought the assertions far from convincing and wasted on so small an audience, but he realized the man was speaking with utter seriousness. And the message was clear. In spite of himself he was especially irritated on one point.

'You make the same damned mistake about me that all of your people do, General,' he protested. 'I don't have my hand out. I earn my way or I buy it. I may be *yanqui*, as you all insist on calling me, but I'm no longer a foreigner. I may not have been carried here in the family womb, like the rest of you, but I came by choice and I came to stay.

'To that degree this is my country as much as it is yours. That's all I want. That's all I ask from any of you.'

'You want too much,' Armijo said shortly. 'We are jealous people. Now, if you'll excuse me—'

The general crossed abruptly to an inner door and disappeared through it. Further irritated by the curt dismissal, Stanton found his way to the street. His original liking for Manuel Armijo was souring rapidly. He began to wonder if he had urged poor counsel upon Felipe Peralta and his fellow *hacendados*. He began to think he should have gone directly to Santa Fe and his private showdown with Royer and Montoya instead of coming here. It would have been a hell of a lot easier on his disposition and the seat of his ass.

He was hungry and located a small *cocina*. As before, his Yankee appearance and dress attracted far more attention than in Santa Fe. Maybe Armijo was right. Maybe what he wanted would take too long. Maybe it would never come about in his time. Maybe he did expect too much.

He felt better after eating. He felt even better after a couple of hours of restless wandering through the streets and alleys of the town. Manuel Armijo's attitude and personality might have changed, but his professionalism had not. Quietly, busily, in small shops and other establishments throughout the town, Albuquerque was preparing to put an army in the field.

Corrals were filling with good horses. In open spaces concealed from general notice, small groups of men were drilling diligently. Supplies were being accumulated in many places in quantities too large for stocks against normal trade. Mexican arms of good quality were being assembled and made ready for use. There was little of the normal workaday chatter so dear to these people. In its place was a subdued air of urgency and anticipation.

General Armijo's declaration of his own purpose may have been too bombastic for Stanton's taste. An unnecessary posturing before the fact. But the general was obviously not permitting any such self-important and swaggering vanity among those who were preparing to accompany him.

Stanton knew well enough that the qualities necessary to inspired leadership varied greatly from period to period and people to people. History taught no other lesson more convincingly. It struck him that Armijo might know exactly the precise blend necessary here and that in point of fact there was a great deal Spencer Stanton had yet to learn about New Mexico and New Mexicans.

In midafternoon he was handed a note on the street. It was an invitation to dine at the general's house. He bought a shirt in the same shop he and Jaime had patronized before and found the Indian bath again. He drew the same old woman and she remembered him. She remarked, as he protested the heat to which she once more subjected him, at how completely and well his wounds had healed.

Obviously he had had the benefit of an Indian cure. He thought of 'Mana's care and solemnly agreed with her that none was its equal. This pleased the old woman and she scented his bath and clothing with some kind of pungent sage as a special dispensation.

The dinner was not the social occasion Stanton anticipated. The others in attendance were Armijo's friends and neighbors, members of his staff. The retaking of Santa Fe was planned in detail at table. Stanton found he was to have an integral part. He was surprised. He had supposed that the general, with his attitude of New Mexico for New Mexicans, would exclude any foreigner he could from participation in his campaign.

The general plan was simple. It was designed specifically to avoid any large-scale confrontation, if at all possible. As Armijo had said before, he didn't want to kill farmers who were better off in their fields. The intent was to seal the city off before attempting to enter it. This would accomplish two purposes. It would prevent the escape of any of the principal rebels and any chance they could continue the revolt

206

elsewhere. Equally important it would shut off any possible reinforcement from outside. To this end the general was dividing his force into three highly mobile parties.

The main body, under Armijo himself, was to proceed directly and openly up the *Camino Real*, cutting Santa Fe off from the south. This was the only threat the rebels must suppose they had to face. Two smaller forces were to operate as flankers. One, under a dour, saber-scarred veteran named De La Rosa, was to follow the east bank of the Rio Grande as far as the mouth of the canyon, cutting into the mountains from there to seal off Santa Fe from the north and west. The other was to hold further east along the foothills of the Sandías and into the Sangre de Cristos to blockade the wagon tracks of the Santa Fe Trail down Glorieta Pass. These two forces were to close in on the city in a pincers movement, reassuring the country people and dispersing any gatherings of consequence. Stanton was assigned command of the Glorieta party, the assumption being that if another freight string came in over the Trail from the States during the campaign, he would best be able to deal with his countrymen.

When the dinner broke up Armijo gave them all warning.

'I want no ambitious and hasty men,' he said. 'The *yanquis* watch us closely these days. The Trail grows shorter with every train of their wagons. They want our trade. If it seems we can't manage our own affairs, they'll come in and manage them for us. That is their way. And we'll have to account for ourselves to Mexico City as well. The *ricos* in the north will support us. *Señor* Stanton brings me assurance of that. I want nothing foolish done. I intend to take Santa Fe without a shot being fired, if at all possible. Let no man forget it.'

Three days later they rode for the City of the Holy Faith.

## CHAPTER SIXTEEN

Night camp was made on the northern edge of the broad flat where Stanton and Jaime had been caught with their burros in the cloudburst. Almost the spot, in fact, where Royer, Hagen, and Brock had turned back with Luis Montoya and his detachment of Governor Pérez' guards.

General Armijo's military competence was evident in the orderly, spartan layout of the camp. His confidence was measured by the small size of his total force. Stanton reckoned it at no more than a hundred and twenty men. Not many with which to disperse a belligerent mob and take a city the size of Santa Fe. But they were well mounted, well disciplined, and well armed.

Except for numbers and lack of standardized uniform, this force had the appearance and cohesiveness of a professional European army. By the end of this first day Stanton was quite impressed and said so. Armijo was pleased at his admiration.

'Some of your countrymen sometimes make a joke of my title,' he said. 'A Mexican army is all generals.'

'They say the same about Indians. They're all chiefs.'

'And I understand yours are all privates. It goes against their grain to issue orders or obey them.'

'Some do carry the idea of personal liberty a little far, all right,' Stanton agreed. 'But they seem to fight pretty well when it comes down to the shooting.'

'So I've read. Most men will when they're fighting for their homes, *señor*. But this is different. We're going against ourselves, our own people. Because government is so far from us here. What the Germans would call a police action. To teach a few wild ones they can't overthrow order and take the law into their own hands, regardless of the wrongs involved.

'Our military men have had to face a lot of that in the last three hundred years, from Yucatán to New Mexico. We've had to learn. I'm a general, but I'd rather have a hundred trained and disciplined men I can trust than regiments of volunteer militia. For this kind of action, understand. The people accept them better. It's a business to them. There are no unnecessary excesses.'

Stanton nodded.

'A civil action's difficult at best,' he admitted. 'We learned that with our people who sided with the British. It takes a long time to live down that kind of bad blood.'

'Exactly what I'm determined to avoid, if I can,' the general said. 'You'll find your men understand that. I want you and Captain De La Rosa to move your detachments out two hours before daylight. Being smaller parties you'll travel a little faster, but I want to be sure you have enough lead time to get into your flanking positions before I come in sight of the city. I believe a direct approach is best, and things are apt to come to a head pretty quickly after that. But wait for word from me before closing in.'

Stanton nodded. Armijo shook hands and started away. Stanton checked him.

'One thing more, General. Exactly why did you put me in charge of the Glorieta party?'

Armijo smiled.

'For appearances, I didn't want a foreigner with my personal party. It might be misunderstood. Such things are important at a time like this. And I knew you'd have your own reasons for insisting on being an active part of the plan. I thought that if I gave you sufficient responsibility you wouldn't ease off at some point and attempt a personal invasion of Santa Fe on your own.'

Stanton laughed.

'Fair enough,' he said. 'I would have, you know, if you'd tried to leave me out.'

*     *     *

The flanking parties, thirty men each, left the sleeping camp at the appointed hour. They separated at once and disappeared from each other into the night. By daylight Stanton's group was into the mountains. It cut the ruts of the Santa Fe Trail on the downslope of Glorieta Pass, near where Stanton had separated from Jaime.

They found no traffic in either direction. Such *paisanos* as they saw were in fields along the bottoms. Stanton thought that the messengers Felipe Peralta sent out had done their work well. The don's friends among the *hacendados* had pulled their people in and reassured them. It appeared that Armijo, if he did not have full support at once, at least would encounter no resistance of consequence from this direction. Stanton hoped Captain De La Rosa was finding the same conditions as he came up from the Rio Grande. It would make the virtually bloodless takeover Armijo was hoping for that much easier.

He kept his men moving in a slow sweep down the pass, searching for any groups that

211

might remain potentially hostile and taking pains to keep word of their approach from running ahead of them. As they rode Stanton waited anxiously for word from below that Armijo was before Santa Fe. After several hours, when he was sure they were already within gunsound of the city and did not dare risk closer approach without orders, he called a halt.

As more time passed and shadows began to lengthen perceptibly, Stanton became more and more concerned that Armijo's messenger had inexplicably missed them, or that something involving the main party had gone seriously wrong. Appointing a second in command with orders to follow cautiously in another hour, Stanton rode on down the Trail.

The valley of the Rio Santa Fe remained as somnolent and silent in the late afternoon sun as it had been the first time he rode into it. When the first faintly pink adobe cubes of the city came in sight, he pulled up again. From this point he had several miles of the course of the *Camino Real* in view, off to the south, and nowhere was there any indication of General Armijo's main party, now alarmingly overdue.

Stanton went on and, as he came among the first houses, he began to encounter a little traffic. No one paid him any attention. He supposed that by now he was as familiar a sight to the people of Santa Fe as some of them were to him. What baffled him was the lack of excitement among them, the undisturbed normal routine.

Obviously no invading army had entered their city in the last few hours and they knew nothing of the existence of such a threat. The whereabouts of Armijo and Captain De La Rosa troubled him deeply. So did the knowledge that his own party from Glorieta would soon follow him in unsuspectingly.

But once into the city unchallenged like this, he couldn't turn back without attempting to discover exactly what the situation here was. The information might be invaluable to Armijo when they were able to link up again. He thought he could risk a few more minutes to get it and still intercept his men in time to prevent collision with the rebels, who must still be holding the *palacio*.

He thought of Sol Wetzel. He would be the quickest and most reliable source of information. He took the alley to the back door of the trader's storeroom. He hammered on it but could raise no one within. Leaving his horse here, he ran lightly to the end of the block, then strolled on casually to the plaza. As he entered the square he saw that the main door of the *palacio*, opposite, was open and that no guards were stationed there, as they had been in Governor Pérez' time. Nor were any in sight on the rest of the square.

The new governor, Gonzales, and his rebels were more confident than their situation warranted. Apparently Manuel Armijo would have the advantage of complete surprise, if he ever showed up. Stanton thought he could risk it and strode on to Wetzel's plaza door. It also was locked. He rattled the latch, hoping the trader was in his little side room over the secret cellar and could hear.

As he did so two men came out of a neighboring shop. With a jolt of astonishment he saw that both were officers in General Armijo's missing main party, men who had attended the dinner at the general's house in Albuquerque. He could not mistake them. They saw him at the same time and moved quickly to him, coming up on either side.

'The general will want to see you,' one murmured. 'Make no difficulty.'

Incredulous, Stanton offered no resistance or protest. They steered him diagonally across the plaza and through the open main door of the *palacio*. It was true. Manuel Armijo sat with his saddle boots up on the big table that had served Albino Pérez as a desk. He had an enormous smile of self-satisfaction and amusement at the astonishment Stanton could not yet shake. He dismissed the two officers who had brought Stanton to him.

'You're a little earlier than I anticipated,' he said. 'I didn't expect you until well after dark. I thought you would wait until sunset before your *yanqui* impatience made you ignore my orders and come on in.'

'What happened?' Stanton asked. 'How did you do it so quickly?'

'A devious man uses devious means if they are at hand,' the general said complacently. 'The same way Gonzales and his rebels did. With a little money. They bought some of Pérez' men to open the doors of the *palacio* to them. I bought some of theirs to do the same for me. The same men. I sent a spy in ahead. They took the bait, and I have taken Santa Fe.'

'Without a shot?'

'No. Nothing is that easy. As I had hoped, we had no resistance coming into the city. Felipe Peralta and his *rico* friends did their work well. And the rebels had done enough harm already. The people liked the looks of my soldiers after the rabble that had been running the streets. They were happy we were here. They knew it meant some kind of order and government again.

'But even after we were in the *palacio*, the rebel ringleaders and their Indian governor holed up in the barracks across the patio. We had to kill a few before the Indian and the rest surrendered. I believe I only had one man wounded.'

'Then you did cut me out of it after all. Deliberately. You never intended to send me a message.'

'Only if things went badly and I needed those thirty men. I told you it was none of your affair.'

215

Stanton shook his head in disbelief.

'But as I came in just now there was no sign of excitement, nothing unusual. Until I saw your two men I had no idea that anybody in town even knew you were anywhere near.'

'Naturally,' Armijo agreed. 'Because I ordered it. Everything back to normal. There has been too much tumult already. Too much time has been lost. Too much trade. Too much fear. It's not good for people to be afraid in their homes and on their own streets. They have to be told that everything is all right again.

'Order them to believe it and they will, at once. That's what good government is. To give orders and make the people believe them. That's what they want anyway. They don't want to find out these things for themselves. They merely want to be told and made to believe.'

Listening to this man, Stanton realized that Armijo had done a great deal of planning toward this day. He knew what he wanted to do and exactly how to do it. The general's almost scornful attitude toward the *paisanos*, the little people, did not sit too well with Stanton's personal notion of the dignity of the individual, but it was paternal in that it was protective, and such protection by government was long overdue here. He thought that odds-on, Manuel Armijo, strongman that he was, would make the province a good

216

governor, once he succeeded in wangling confirmation in office from Mexico City.

It pleased Stanton that this conclusion was important to him. Not that he expected personal benefit. He did not. He supposed that, as a Yankee and a foreigner, he would always be at some disadvantage with Armijo. The man could no more change in that regard than he could himself. But some clarification of his own position was now in order.

If he was to understand the general, then Armijo must understand him completely. If he was not to have the full sympathy of the government in what he intended to do, then the government should know precisely what reaction to anticipate should disagreements occur, now and in the future. All fair men could only operate in this fashion.

'You say you bought your way into the *palacio* today, General,' he said. 'Through the same men the rebels hired to help dislodge Governor Pérez.'

'Yes,' Armijo agreed. 'It's time we talked of them. That's why I asked to have you brought to me as soon as you showed up. Friends of yours.'

'Bennett Royer and Luis Montoya? Hardly!'

'Of course. A misused word. But known to you. And there are three now. Another *yanqui*, but recently recovered from a gunshot wound.'

Stanton swore softly.

'Paul Hagen. I was afraid of that. I might as

217

well tell you straight out, General, I may have to kill them or give them their chance to kill me. I want no interference in whatever I have to do.'

'There is that much of importance between you?'

'There will be if they stay in New Mexico.'

Armijo sighed.

'One can always hope otherwise until one is sure. I paid them off as soon as the prisoners were taken. With that and what they collected for the head of Albino Pérez, they should be satisfied. I gave them fair warning. It's all I felt obliged to do. I gave them four hours to get out of Santa Fe.

'Not an official order, understand. After all, they did render a service to the government. Just personal advice. I warned them that some time after four hours you would be here and I couldn't guarantee their safety. That's the real reason I didn't send you the message you expected when we entered the city. I promised them that time.'

'They're still here?'

Armijo shrugged.

'Under the circumstances they'd be extremely foolish to let me know.'

'The time you promised them is up?'

Armijo nodded. Stanton came reluctantly to his feet. He drew the Navy Colt and spun the cylinder, making sure all of the caps were in place.

'No interference?' he asked.

'Go with God,' Manuel Armijo answered. 'A man must deal with his enemies in his own fashion.'

## CHAPTER SEVENTEEN

As Stanton stepped out onto the portico across the front of the *Palacio de los Gobernadores*, a hand touched his arm. It was Wetzel.

'Didn't figure I'd better break in on you,' the trader said, indicating the *palacio*. 'By the time I got my door open they'd already started across with you. Seemed best to wait here. Where the hell you been?'

'Albuquerque, with a message from Felipe Peralta. Riding with the general. The foxy bastard left me with a party to cool my heels out on Glorieta until this show was over.'

'You're a damned fool to come in openly like you did. Royer and Montoya are in town. Paul Hagen's with them.'

'I know. That's why I'm here.'

Wetzel laid hold of Stanton's arm again.

'Come on. I got to talk to you.'

'Later,' Stanton said impatiently.

Wetzel's grip tightened insistently.

'The hell with that!' he snapped with impatience of his own. 'Save that for later. You can always get yourself killed. Don't draw a hand until you know what the odds are and what's on the table for stakes.'

Common sense told Stanton the advice was good. He was letting himself be hurried. That was dangerous. He had intended to see Wetzel in the first place. His own convictions notwithstanding, it was possible there might be another way to deal with Bennett Royer and his partners.

'All right,' he said.

They crossed the plaza. As Wetzel was unlocking his door a mounted troop rode into the square at a sharp trot.

'Now what?' the trader demanded with a touch of alarm.

'The rest of Armijo's men,' Stanton told him. 'Following me in from where I left them on the Trail.'

'Some men are sure shot in the ass with luck,' Wetzel snorted. 'Put them all together and it sure isn't much of an army!'

'It did the trick,' Stanton answered. 'Like Armijo knew it would. Don't make any mistake about that. He never plays to luck.'

Wetzel grunted unintelligibly and they entered the store. The trader locked the door behind them and led the way to his spartan, one-room quarters. He lit the lamp in the dark, windowless cell and offered a bottle. Stanton declined. Wetzel swallowed a healthy slug.

'I needed that,' he growled. He sank down on the cot and put the bottle on the floor between his feet.

'Sometimes I think I'm a pretty smart boy, Stanton,' he continued, 'then again I'm not too damned sure. Know what you said about the general being a foxy bastard? Let me tell you what actually started this revolt. It was that jack-string of wool he sent up here on consignment to me.

'Governor Pérez was sore as hell about it. Mostly because Armijo had something to do with it, I think. So he slapped that tax against the wool on everything moving in the city. Of course he had to make it apply to everyone and everything else, too. That really fixed the wagon.'

The trader took another healthy slug from the bottle and shook his head.

'The thought strikes me that Armijo sent that wool up here on purpose, that he'd of kept on sending it till poor Pérez blew up. I think he encouraged the hell out of the rebels when they got upset over another tax, on top of everything else.

'Sure, Pérez had been squeezing everybody dry for a long time. We all knew that. It had gotten pretty desperate for everybody, all along the line. But I think Armijo let that Indian assassinate Pérez and set himself up as governor just so the general could march up here, clean house, and move in himself. How's that strike you?'

'The thought has occurred to me,' Stanton

221

admitted.

'Well, he's a hell of a businessman is all I can say,' Wetzel growled, not without admiration. 'But it's that wool I wanted to talk to you about. I sent it on as soon as the rebels took over and things quieted down a little. We're going to make out good on it. Now the general tells me there's plenty more where that came from, and no taxes. We got a brand new business going for ourselves, man.'

'That's your end.'

'I know. The Corona Grant's yours. But you want to lose that too? Everything. The works. That's what'll happen if you force Royer and his sidekicks to a showdown or let them force you. Maybe they won't figure out a way to get their hands on what you've started. Maybe they don't want it. Maybe they just want a free shot at anything else they can pick up out here. What the hell difference does it make to you if you're dead?'

'Some men are enemies simply because they're different, Sol,' Stanton said, stating a firm conviction. 'What do you think most wars are about? You know these men. Everything they've done since they got here shows it. What they've done before they'll do again. They won't change. Can't, in fact.'

'That's your responsibility?'

'Sooner or later they'll have to destroy me or I'll have to destroy them. This is my country now. I'll not have them in it. I can't afford to.'

Wetzel hunched forward eagerly.

'Wait a minute! Let me get this straight. You want them out of New Mexico. That's all?'

'That's all.'

'Then, for God's sake, let somebody tell them that's all there is to it before some damned fool thing happens and you wind up with a bullet in the head!'

'General Armijo already has.'

'He ordered them out of Mexico?' Wetzel asked hopefully.

Stanton rose, impatience beginning to surge in him again.

'He refused to do that. Just a personal suggestion. And they're already past the deadline.'

'He won't interfere further?'

'No.'

'Damn it,' Wetzel said desperately. 'Doesn't he see what they're up to? They're human. They're trying some kind of a stupid bluff. Trying to crack you down. Push you off balance. Into something you can't handle alone. But they got to see they're playing a long shot, too. Let somebody else talk to them. Hell, let me!'

Stanton felt again a tug of warmth toward the shrewd little trader, who had boasted he was a coward. He knew now why Wetzel had wanted those two stiff jolts of Taos Lightning.

'It's all yours if you want it, partner,' he said. 'I wish you luck, and I mean that. This sure isn't something I want to do. But I will if I have to. I'll be in the La Fonda tavern for an hour. If they're not on their way by then, I'll come looking for them.'

'You don't give a fella much time!' Wetzel complained. 'Let's go.'

He grabbed up his hat and let them back out onto the plaza. He hurried away so intently on his errand that he neglected to lock the door of his store. Stanton hung the lock through the hasp and snapped it closed for him.

Santa Fe's evening promenade was beginning. It was now enlivened by a number of General Armijo's Albuquerque *soldados*, unabashedly eyeing the girls in competition with the local talent. The street shutters across the face of the tavern in the plaza corner of La Fonda had already been folded back.

Stanton took the table he had occupied before, his back to a wall and his angle such that he had a clear view of both the promenaders in the plaza and the main room of the tavern. There was little trade at this early hour, but four of General Armijo's men followed him in and found a table to their liking.

They nodded at Stanton in passing. He was momentarily amused. Comrades in arms. It was not as difficult for a *yanqui* to win a place in this country as its natives maintained. Turning his head to look out over the promenaders in the plaza, he noted that in the background, across the corner of the square, the main door of the *Palacio de los Gobernadores* still gaped wide, open to all comers.

Stanton did not anticipate a long wait. He wanted a drink to span it. Instead he ordered a *chocolate*. He sipped this and thought of what might lie ahead. He had told Wetzel the truth. He did wish the trader luck. He had no taste for this sort of thing. Only once before had he known in advance that he might kill a man, that his own peace of mind and perhaps survival depended upon it. He had failed that opportunity.

That man had lived to destroy Spencer Stanton by reputation, to strip him of family, friends, and possessions, and in a final humiliating arrogance, to marry the faithless wife he had seduced. He still lived. It would not happen again. The stakes were greater here. Far more important. This was the beginning, not the end.

He finished the *chocolate*. The taste lingered cloyingly in his mouth. More interior tables began to fill up. He wished suddenly that he had not chosen so public a place. The thought was merely an involuntary working of his mind. He tried to control it. When someone came to him it might be only Sol Wetzel, smiling that the others were gone and it was over as simply as that.

Nevertheless he moved his table a little so that there was a trifle more open space about it

225

and a few aisles in which bystanders would be clear of the line of fire.

The hour he had specified was long up, and yet Stanton had not been able to force himself to begin his promised search when they appeared. He realized they had run the time out deliberately. Wetzel was not with them, so he knew what the answer was to be. Still, a man did what had to be done in his own fashion. He put both hands on the table before him, where they were plainly visible to all. But he let them lie at ease and did not clasp them.

All three wore pistols, preferring to have them loosely thrust through the belt to the left of the buckle than stuck in a pocket or holster. The weapons were the common big Spanish doubles, their big slugs, almost certainly lethal with any reasonable placement, but necessarily most effective at short range. Stanton thought this choice also had been deliberate. It was to be close work.

They came via the main quarters of La Fonda, separating immediately as they entered the tavern, diagonally across from Stanton's position. All carefully avoided the clear aisles Stanton had noted earlier, using other patrons for cover as much as possible as they advanced individually. And they moved with cool confidence according to a prearranged plan. Stanton realized that each in his own way knew a great deal about this kind of thing.

The room quickly sensed the intent of the

entry and the identity of the intended victim. In many small movements those thinking themselves endangered tried to shift to safer positions without attracting attention. Armijo's four soldiers, perhaps more experienced in such situations, remained as they were, upright in their seats and tensely immobile.

The sudden interior tenseness communicated itself to the plaza. Promenaders came to a halt in a breathless kind of half awareness and anticipation. Beyond them out of the corner of his eye, Stanton saw a man appear in the main doorframe of the *palacio*. He thought it was Manuel Armijo.

The three came on through the tavern with no heed for any soul in Santa Fe but Spencer Stanton.

Paul Hagen kept boring to the right toward the most difficult and awkward angle of fire from Stanton's position. Under any other circumstance Stanton would not have recognized the man. He had wasted away to half his weight. His flesh was wholly without color. He moved in a painful half crouch, twisted a little to one side, but he moved lightly, easily, and with grim determination. His malevolence was an aura from which others shrank visibly as he passed.

Luis Montoya, with an ex-soldier's directness, came straight toward Stanton down the center of the room. His enmity seemed detached and professional, without the fire in Paul Hagen's eyes. Considering Montoya's longer practice and greater familiarity with the Spanish weapons they had chosen, Stanton thought he would be the fastest and the most skilled and accurate in their use.

Bennett Royer, only a few feet to the left of Montoya, offered the best target because of his size. He seemed as cool and dispassionate as Montoya, but Stanton knew men of his build and bulk could seldom move as swiftly as their lighter and more wiry counterparts. And the man still limped from the bullet Jaime had put into him at Mora. In terms of timing he thought that Royer would be the slowest in getting a shot away.

His greatest concern was Hagen, now far to the right. He knew he could not free his own weapon and turn at that awkward angle necessary to fire first at Hagen without giving Montoya and possibly even Royer too much advantage. Therefore he planned the only course he could, knowing that for an unavoidable instant or two, while his shoulder was turned to fire fairly at Royer and Montoya, Hagen would be practically behind him with an open target and nothing to hurry his shot.

Stanton did not see the signal, yet one was given. All three jerked their guns free simultaneously. At the first twitch of movement by Montoya, Stanton slapped for his gun and powerfully kicked his table away, trying to make an advantage of his awkward, seated position.

The table flew into the air, blocking out Montoya for an instant and taking his first shot. As Stanton went over backward in his chair from the force of his kick, he had an instant's clear view of Royer and risked a snap shot in motion. He hit the man but could not tell how hard.

Crashing to the floor on his back in the splinters of his chair, Stanton somersaulted backward, feet over head, and surged up with his back against the wall, facing Royer. He saw that Royer was still on his feet, a little blood on his cheek, his pistol seeking its target. Stanton shot him again and saw the man shudder. Royer's pistol fired into the floor.

With one barrel of his weapon empty, Luis Montoya was taking time to make sure with his remaining charge. In the same sweep of continuous movement, pivoting swiftly on shoulders pinned firmly against the wall behind him, Stanton fired at the Mexican. Montoya's second barrel let go just as the ball from the Navy Colt struck the embroidered pocket of his shirt, and the slug from the big Spanish pistol went wild.

At the same moment, from the far right as Stanton had feared, Paul Hagen fired his unhurried first shot. Only Stanton's continuing spinning motion saved him. The big slug struck the wall at his ear with a blinding explosion of fragmented adobe. Half stunned by the concussion of so near a miss and half blinded, he staggered out from the wall, turning desperately toward Hagen when he knew it was already too late.

Gunsound came again, ringing in his ears, but Stanton remained untouched. Pawing the grit from his eyes, he saw Hagen jerking and turning slowly on his toes like a marionette on a string, his body literally being torn to pieces. Three tables away the Armijo men who had followed Stanton in here from the plaza, his comrades in arms on the march on Santa Fe, lowered their pistols as Hagen's body slumped to the floor.

In the sudden hushed silence Stanton heard his name being called frantically. It was Wetzel, running through the tables from the La Fonda entrance. His hat was missing. Blood was oozing from a big welt above his ear. He rushed up to Stanton.

'Thank God, Stanton! You all right?'

Stanton nodded. Someone righted the overturned table and pushed up chairs. They sank down. Stanton saw the table top bore a deep gouge where Montoya's first bullet had struck. Wetzel looked with aversion at the bodies on the floor and fingered the gash in his scalp.

'So help me, I'll never argue with you again,' he said. 'I found them in a La Fonda back room. The bastards never even listened to me. Just waited the time out, knocked me in the head so I couldn't warn you, and came after you. They deserve what they got.'

Stanton nodded absently, his attention on something else. General Armijo was approaching. The growing crowd in the plaza deferentially parted to let him through. The general looked impersonally at the bodies and nodded approval to the four soldiers who had sided with Stanton at the last moment when Hagen had him cold.

'You obeyed your orders well,' the general said. 'Search them.'

The soldiers knelt over the dead men and began going through their pockets. Armijo came to the table occupied by Wetzel and Stanton. He signaled a waiter and sat down to join them. Fingering the gouge in the table top, he shook his head.

'They wouldn't listen to reason, eh?'

'Did you expect them to?' Stanton asked.

'No,' the general admitted candidly.

The soldiers brought over the results of their search. It made a substantial heap of gold coins on the table.

'Thieves, murderers, traitors,' Armijo said. 'Did they think I would let them leave New Mexico with this much gold from the treasury—or let such rotten rascals stay, alive?'

'So you let me be your executioner,' Stanton accused.

'You must admit it will look better in Mexico City,' Armijo answered. 'A quarrel between foreigners. But I did arrange help if you needed it, *señor*.'

He indicated the four soldiers.

'Comrades in arms, my eye!' Stanton muttered.

'I'm afraid I don't understand,' Armijo said politely.

'It's all right. I do.'

Out in the plaza a drumroll sounded.

'The official hour of sunset,' Armijo said. 'We will have a good view from here.'

Along a narrow side street from behind the *palacio*, a small spit-and-polish military detachment marched smartly into the plaza. In their midst was a small huddle of bare-foot, half-naked prisoners, their wrists lashed together behind their backs.

Against a blank, pockmarked stretch of the thick walls of the old fortress, these miserable few were lined up facing the expectant crowd now jamming the plaza, without benefit of benediction or blindfold. Their military escort wheeled briskly and came to a halt, a precise in-line file facing their charges at twenty paces.

At command muskets at present arms leaped to shoulder and delivered a shattering volley. The figures against the wall of the *palacio* buckled and slumped to the ground. The drumroll stopped. Manuel Armijo thrust his feet out before him at the tavern table and looked at Stanton.

'A necessary discipline,' he said. 'You see, I, too, know how to deal with my enemies, *señor*. One of those was José Gonzales, the Indian who dared to call himself the governor of New Mexico.'

Sol Wetzel closed his eyes for a moment, then reopened them, shaking his head.

'General,' he said with considerable conviction, 'you are a son of a bitch.'

Before Armijo could react to this questionable compliment, the trader picked up the glass that had been set before him and in a surprisingly graceful and unquestionably sincere gesture of toast added:

'Long live the new governor—'

Not in the least offended, Armijo repeated the gesture.

'I'll drink to that,' he said.

The two drained their glasses.

Spencer Stanton left his untouched.


## CHAPTER EIGHTEEN

Impatient to be home, liking the word and the feeling accompanying the thought, Stanton crossed El Cumbre for the third time. Again he was trailing a pair of laden packhorses. Emerging from the mountains he turned urgently north onto the Corona. Others could carry word of Armijo's easy triumph at Santa Fe to Rancho Mora. Felipe Peralta would learn of it soon enough and Stanton was too expectant to take the detour necessary to reach his neighbor.

Long before he had the camp on the Corona in view, a rider raced down the slope of a distant hill toward him, riding with wild Ute abandon. It was 'Mana. It never failed to astonish Stanton that a people who had possessed horses no more than ten or twelve generations should have so quickly become such superb horsemen, and she the most magnificent of all. He wondered how many days, how many hours she had spent riding to some high place, like the one she was descending from now, to watch and wait for his return.

Stanton pulled up and dismounted, leaving his horses to crop the thick, soft grass underfoot. 'Mana came on like the wind, hair flying, skirt kited to her knees, her body moving gracefully with the powerful reach of the horse. She flung down yards away, while her horse was still in motion, and ran into Stanton's arms, as the abandoned horse trotted over to join the others.

There were tears on her cheeks but happiness was pouring from her. She said nothing. Their bodies met and then their lips. They rocked together precariously then sank slowly together, of one accord, into the sweet grass. They lay there in the warm afternoon sun, the earth of their own domain beneath them, until the hurt of separation and uncertainty was burned away and only the peace of togetherness remained.

They laughed together when they discovered that the cropping horses had had time to drift unnoticed nearly a quarter of a mile away. It was all right. The horses had drifted in the right direction. They followed afoot, hand in hand, and caught them up again.

'Mana teased to know the contents of the packs, what gift he had brought her. Stanton refused, insisting she must wait until they were home. She pretended to pout but was laughing again as they remounted and rode on, side by side.

Presently they came to where the cattle were grazing. Stanton was startled to see the two young Mora bulls again among them.

'We came out one morning and there they were,' 'Mana said. 'Would you believe it? Each had a ribbon around his neck, tied in a bow.'

'Don Felipe?'

'Mana nodded happily.

'Our wedding gift, I think. Father Frederico must have brought them up on his way back to Taos.'

Jaime was sitting his horse on a knoll above the cattle, one knee casually crooked around the horn of his saddle, as though he had been riding herd on beef stock on this grass all of his life. He trotted unhurriedly down to join them.

'Why such an all-fired hurry about getting back?' he complained mischievously to Stanton. 'I like working for a lady boss.'

'No discipline, that's why,' Stanton told him. 'I can tell she's already let you get clean out of hand.'

Jaime grinned. He took up the packhorse leads and they rode on.

Stanton could not believe the camp on the creek. The original brush shelter had been strengthened and improved. It now served as a kitchen and storage place, with sleeping space for Jaime. The large double-roofed wall tent with airspace between the two flies, which had been in the first pack loads he brought up from Wetzel's store, was tautly set on the opposite side of the fire-ring. A fresh bed, comfortably large enough for two, was made up on the clean canvas floor. 'Mana's things were there. So were Stanton's, cozily intermingled, as should be.

Back of the tent a sufficient distance for modesty and convenience was a serviceable brush outhouse, light enough to be easily moved as occasion required. 'Mana and Jaime had taken the horses on several trips up to the aspen groves on the mountains and dragged down enough slim, straight poles to put up a small corral for the horses on the bank of the creek, a few yards downstream.

'Of course we can't stay here when deep

winter comes,' 'Mana said, delighted with his approval. 'Not in a tent. But we'll be comfortable till then. Afterward there's the ruin of a small old Spanish house in a little canyon above the Cimarron, a few miles from here. It could be made usable, I think.'

Jaime nodded agreement.

'I rode up there with her one day. Not in too bad shape at all. I think it must have been in use up until fairly recently. We could get by fine.'

'Unless it is your wish to go back to your own country,' 'Mana suggested.

Stanton had already marked the improvement in communication between 'Mana and the boy. Both were unself-consciously experimenting with the opposing basics of Spanish and English, casually intermixing simple words and phrases as they mastered them. This, with an imaginative combination of a kind of sign language and some lively charades, sometimes produced hilarious and unanticipated results, but an exchange of sorts was possible and seemed to suffice.

Stanton was not ready to tell them what his own intentions and plans for winter were. This was part of his big surprise and he wanted to delay it a little longer in anticipation of their excitement.

'This is my country now,' was all he would say. 'We stay.'

Instead he gave them a full account of his

errand to General Armijo in Albuquerque and subsequent events at Santa Fe. They were especially intrigued by his impressions of Armijo. Both agreed that the wily general promised a good governorship. That was good news. But the best was that Stanton's final confrontation with Royer, Montoya, and Hagen had come and gone. That was over. Now he had no enemies.

They cooked supper and ate in the twilight. Stanton opened the packs he had brought. Besides supplies and additional gear there were a few gifts, as 'Mana had teased to know.

New jacket, pants, shirt, and boots for Jaime. A full, ground-length, embroidered Spanish dress and tiny shoes for 'Mana. Both went into their respective shelters and put these new clothes on at once. 'Mana reappeared fit for a ball in the *palacio* at Santa Fe—tall, full-formed, and regal, with no trace of her ancestry apparent in this European garb. She giggled at the way she teetered uncertainly on the unaccustomed lift of the new shoes and took them off. But she held them in her lap when she sat down, running her hands over their shining polish and fragile, delicate shape.

'You're not to be trusted away,' she accused. 'When will I ever wear such things?'

'Soon enough,' Stanton promised.

She laughed at him.

'My mother warned me when I was very young that I would marry an impractical man.'

He did not think he had heard her mention a member of her family before. Again he wanted to know more about them, more about what she had been like when she was a child.

He showed her the new saddle to replace the bare, worn tree of the Indian one she rode. He handed Jaime the light Kentucky rifle Wetzel had taken in from some trapper or freighter in pawn. It was not the equal of his own Henry, but it was serviceable and the rifling was cleanly cut and bright. It would shoot well. The boy held it with as much care as 'Mana did her shoes.

Finally Stanton could contain himself no longer. He brought out the oilskin packet that had been handed to him by Albino Pérez' clerk under the portico of the *Palacio de los Gobernadores*. 'Mana had waited long enough to know.

'Do you read?' he asked her gently.

'Father Frederico would be insulted to hear you ask that,' she laughed. 'Such a time as he had with me at first. What is it?'

'My wedding present to you.'

She unwrapped the packet with tantalizing care, folding out the crisp documents it contained. She read them rapidly, her breathing rising quickly in tempo as she did so. She gave Stanton a strange look and reread them slowly and carefully. He waited patiently until she was finished. When she said nothing, did nothing but just sit there, he became anxious.

'Do you understand what it is, what it means?'

She nodded, her head down. He saw there were tears on her cheeks again, dripping unheeded onto the vellum sheets in her hands.

'You—you've bought the grant,' she said with difficulty. 'You want it that much—love it that much. You own legal title to the Corona.'

'We do,' he corrected. 'You love it too. Now it's ours. Spencer and 'Mana Stanton, a man and wife.'

She raised her head slowly, her eyes glistening.

'Why didn't you tell me?' she asked softly. 'When you came back the first time. You'd already done it then.'

Spencer Stanton smiled at her.

'Because I wanted you to marry a man, not a *yanqui* with two hundred thousand acres of land. I had to know I had something more than that to offer you first.'

She continued to look at him in that strange way. Jaime, apparently sensing that this was no time to express the high excitement dancing in his eyes at such great news, quietly rose with his new rifle and disappeared into the brush shelter. 'Mana still remained motionless and silent. Stanton felt a twinge of astonished disappointment. Absently, without taking her eyes from his face. 'Mana slowly refolded the vellum documents and returned them to their oilskin cover.

'What's the matter?' he finally asked. 'Aren't you excited—happy?'

'Mana let the packet slide from her lap unnoticed, came across to him on her knees through the dirt in her new dress, and threw her arms about him, clinging tightly with all her strength.

'I have no words,' she whispered. 'I think I have to go to bed with you. Right now. Quickly. I think I can tell you then. I think then you'll know.'

*　　*　　*

Stanton showed 'Mana and Jaime the branding iron a smith had made for him in Santa Fe. Pressed into the wet sand on the creekbank, it left the clear impression of a simplified royal crown. One by one they caught up, threw, and branded the Corona beeves and the two Mora bulls, so that their ownership could be recognized by anyone, even at some distance.

Stanton could not bring himself to inflict so large a mark on the horses. He burned the same brand in dollar size on the hip of each with the point of a heated knife. 'Mana protested that he was going to insist upon the same indelible mark of his ownership, and in the same place, on Jaime and herself as well. He threw her onto the ground on her belly when the knife was hot,

241

threatening to lift her skirt and do just that. But the teasing was justified. Only he could know the tremendous satisfaction and vanity he drew from seeing that crown on Corona possessions.

The stock recovered from the fleeting indignity of branding and continued to prosper. Jaime hunted with his new rifle and brought in game as the table required. When there were no other chores, he spent long hours with the grazing cattle. Just because he liked to watch them, he explained. Wherever Stanton rode, 'Mana rode beside him in her new saddle.

One day, far out on the grass, she showed him a small, cut stone monument. When they tramped down the growth about it, he discovered a weathered Spanish inscription bearing the date '27 July 1693.' The stone marked the northeast corner of the Corona Grant. In time the other boundaries could be determined by reference to this stone with the use of a map Governor Pérez had taken from the original archives and included in Stanton's packet of documents.

Capping the sidewall of a draw, close in, they later found an outcropping of warm red sandstone flag, which cleaved naturally in four-inch slabs and could be readily cut. Stanton and Jaime began shaping blocks and dragging them into the camp on a boat made of aspen poles—left over from the corral—and drawn by saddle ropes. When there were enough blocks for a start, Stanton began laying them up with clay from a good bed on the creek.

This was his answer to the coming winter. A big, stone-walled, flagstone-floored room, with smaller rooms at either end, built stout and comfortable to last as long as the Corona itself. From this the great house of which he dreamed for 'Mana could grow as time permitted and need required. They moved the brush shelter a few yards so the foundations could sit exactly where he had lain when he first saw the great basin of the grant.

'Mana grew as excited as he as the lines of the walls began to take shape. She puddled clay with her bare feet, treading in strong-stemmed dry grass as a binder, while Jaime cut stone and boated it in. It was a time of accomplishment and content such as Stanton had never known. The permanence he wanted was here and he could feel it as he sweat in the sun.

The dog days of late summer passed. The first chill of fall was in the early morning air, the highest aspen on the slopes of the mountains were beginning to turn, and the thick, stone walls of the house were about four-feet high when Jaime rode back from the quarry without a boat of stone behind him. He was riding fast.

For the first time in many tranquil weeks, Stanton felt a tug of apprehension. He left his work and walked out to meet the boy. 'Mana left her puddled clay and hurried after him.

Jaime wore a worried frown as he rode up.

'Company,' he announced tersely. And he pointed.

To the southeast, from the direction of the wagon road to Santa Fe, a considerable body of horsemen was moving smartly toward them.

'Mexicans,' 'Mana said. 'Not *yanquis*. You'll forgive me if I say thank God to that.'

Stanton noted the tight formation of the riders.

'Soldiers,' he said.

'What's it mean?' Jaime asked.

'I don't know,' Stanton answered quietly.

He went into the tent and buckled on his gun, bringing the Henry rifle with him. When he emerged 'Mana was smiling with relief.

'*Mira!*' she said, pointing as Jaime had, but toward the west, toward the mountains.

Coming up out of a draw that had concealed their approach, another party was rapidly coming on, closer at hand. They were unmistakable, Ute warriors. With relief of his own, Stanton saw Chato among them.

'What the hell?' Jaime suddenly gasped involuntarily.

Stanton turned along the boy's line of sight. Coming in from the south, below his grazing cattle, was yet another group of purposeful riders. The *vaqueros* of Rancho Mora, led by Abelardo the wolf and accompanied by Don Felipe Peralta himself.

The Utes arrived first. Their chief was

Chato's uncle. Stanton thought it was essentially the same band that had raided the wagon train for horses. As Chato hurried toward him the others dismounted and quickly took positions within the rising walls of the stone house.

'We saw them miles out and thought you might need help,' Chato said.

'Any idea who they are, where they're from?'

Chato shrugged.

'White men. They all look the same.'

Mora arrived. Abelardo pulled up at the edge of the camp and remained with his men. Don Felipe dismounted and came on to the tent alone.

'*Señora*,' he said with a little bow to 'Mana. He smiled at Chato before turning to Stanton. 'You have good neighbors, *amigo*.'

'Looks like we may need them,' Stanton said, indicating the approaching military party.

'Possibly,' Don Felipe agreed. 'That's Manuel Armijo. Making an official tour of this part of the province, now that Mexico City has confirmed him as governor. Redressing the wrongs of his predecessors, he says. When we learned he intended to come here, we thought it wise to do the same. One is never sure how fairly he'll deal with a *yanqui*.'

'We'll soon find out,' Stanton said. 'We're grateful, whatever happens. I apologize for our limited hospitality, but we might as well be

245

comfortable.'

He placed a seat for the old don before the tent. Peralta sat down. Stanton joined him. 'Mana, her feet and legs still caked with cláy, sat with them. Jaime handed his rifle to Chato and took up Stanton's Henry from where he had set it aside. Stanton nodded permission to him and the two boys joined the group.

From out on the grass the muted drumming of approaching hoofbeats grew ominously louder.

# CHAPTER NINETEEN

General Armijo prudently halted his fifty or sixty well-armed and proficient *soldados* a few yards short of the perimeter of the camp, from where they had a clear command of the Utes, behind the breast-high walls of the new house, and the wolf of Mora and his *vaqueros*. Stanton did not at all care for the situation. There was not a sufficiently clear-cut balance of power. Mistakes were easily made under such conditions.

Without halting when his men did, the general rode arrogantly on into the group before the tent and remained in his saddle looking down on them.

'Well,' he said to Stanton, 'it seems you've made a liar out of me when I told you that you'd buy no friends here.'

'He has earned them,' Felipe Peralta said quietly. 'I should think your friendship as well, General.'

'Governor,' Armijo corrected, a little testily. 'There is a difference, Don Felipe.'

'Perhaps,' Peralta agreed. 'That remains to be seen. Be so good as to tell us what business brings on this military invasion.'

'I defer to your age and infirmity,' Armijo answered shortly, 'but my business is with this *yanqui* foreigner. And I remind you I have come in person when I could merely have sent out an order.'

He dismounted and indicated the seated circle before the tent.

'Am I invited to join you or must I conclude I am an enemy here and have another armed rebellion on my hands?'

Knowing Armijo's deviousness and the degree to which his power was now consolidated, Stanton felt instinctively wary and uneasy. He wished Peralta would tread a little easier until they could learn the general's purpose, but he knew the old don's pride would permit no compromise. He nodded to Jaime, who brought a supply box from the kitchen shelter for the new governor's use. Armijo seated himself upon it.

'It would be wise to put aside your guns,' he said to Stanton. 'My men know what targets to take first. The woman and the boy included.'

The governor indicated 'Mana and Jaime. Stanton did not care for this kind of coercion. It was not called for. He tapped the holster of the Navy Colt.

'Then I'm afraid New Mexico would have a very short-lived governor, Excellency. You've seen what this can do at odds similar to these. Since you choose to come upon my land as a hostile trespasser rather than an invited guest, I suggest you be very careful. State your business and get the hell out.'

'If we choose not to be gentlemen,' Armijo said with a touch of smugness, 'I can be equally direct. This land you boast about so touchingly is not in fact your land at all. You hold fraudulent title to this grant and I come prepared to evict you from it, by force if necessary.'

'*Cagada!*' 'Mana spat angrily. 'He paid the money and has the papers to prove it, signed by the governor himself.'

'The former governor, my stupid little spitfire,' Armijo corrected imperturbably. 'Once removed, at that. Understand me, all of you. Before you take some unwise action you'll all regret. In recent weeks I have had to take many steps that gave me no pleasure. But justice must be restored. Albino Pérez was an enemy of the people.'

'He was the legally appointed governor of the province, sent here by Mexico City,' Peralta said.

'The fact remains that he was a bandit, Don Felipe, a fact you well know yourself.'

'For the treasury, perhaps. For the government. There is much to be done here by the government when there is money to get it done. For that, maybe. Not for himself.'

'Despite your touching loyalty,' Armijo told the old don, 'when I took office I found private records that Pérez confiscated the vast properties of a defenseless woman, alone in the world, and callously sold them for a few American dollars to this *yanqui* profiteer.'

Armijo turned to Stanton.

'If I seem angry, *señor*, I am. But at the injustice. I don't charge you with any guilt. I recognize your good intentions, as stated to me on more than one occasion. I see cattle out there that I assume must belong to you. I see what you have already accomplished here. It troubles me that all this must come to nothing.

'I am not insensible of the fact that at considerable risk and inconvenience to yourself you have recently rendered valuable services to me and to the cause of government. But as I made clear to you at the time, no personal gratitude or regard can intrude upon my public responsibilities. Possession of this grant must be returned to its true owner.'

'Who is this owner?' 'Mana demanded. 'This woman who's being so unjustly victimized.'

'One Maria Dolores y Jesús Romana Ruíz de Herrera, a childless woman without spouse

249

or surviving family,' Armijo answered. 'So the record reads.'

'Where is she?' 'Mana insisted. 'Is she still alive?'

'It is her interests that I must protect first, *señorita*,' the governor protested mildly. 'There is no record of her death. She can be found.'

'Then find her! Show her to me. Face to face. Prove that she exists now or ever did.'

'Mana had leaped to her feet and was leaning over the seated governor almost threateningly. He blinked at her heat but held his ground firmly.

'That's not the necessary thing now. Time enough later. You don't understand.'

'I understand this,' 'Mana said intensely. 'You'd tear down everything Spencer Stanton is trying to build here for an outdated entry in a book of musty old records. I've ridden every coulee and canyon of the Corona since I was old enough to sit a pony. So have the Utes. Ask Chato there. It belongs to them as much as to any woman. Who is this Maria Ruíz that she has a right to two hundred thousand *yanqui* acres of land?'

She straightened proudly and swept her arm out to encompass the basin.

'Has she ever been on the Corona? Has she climbed as high as she could into the mountains, just to look down on it? What has she ever done to improve it, to make it live? Are

250

her dreams here? Is her blood and sweat on the ground? That's what it takes to possess a land like this. That's what it takes to own it. What woman alone could do that—any woman? I won't have any more talk of your paper justice!'

Stanton had heard that some of the horse Indians were among the greatest and most inspired orators in the world. Now he believed it. 'Mana was magnificent. Chato and Jaime, and even old Don Felipe, were enrapt, as though it was the Corona, the land itself, that had spoken. Manuel Armijo was not.

'Muzzle the woman,' he snapped.

Stanton leaned forward and tugged at the seam of 'Mana's skirt. She stepped back obediently, her breast heaving with the intensity of her feeling, and stood defiantly and protectively above him. He looked at Chato, then at Chato's uncle and the nameless, bow-armed Utes, 'Mana's friends, who were ready to defend him behind the half-finished walls of what was to have been the beginning of 'Mana's great house.

He looked at Abelardo, the wolf of Mora, and his *vaqueros*, ready to stand with their Yankee neighbor. He looked at Felipe Peralta and Jaime and again up at 'Mana herself. His shoulders sagged and he lowered his head. Too many were at stake. He could not risk them because he knew he could not win. So did Governor Armijo.

'Of course the price you paid will be returned,' the governor was saying placatingly. 'There is a record and the unfortunate Pérez couldn't take the gold with him. Not where he went.'

Stanton nodded and rose heavily.

'Turn it over to Sol Wetzel on the plaza,' he said. 'Tell him I'll be down in a few days. I'll fight you, Governor. I'll fight you every step of the way from Santa Fe to Mexico City.'

Armijo also came to his feet.

'As you wish.' He shrugged. 'It's useless, you know. You have my sympathy, but understand I am no different from anyone else in our government, including *el presidente* himself. You stand no chance. You are *yanqui*.'

'I'll be down in a few days,' Stanton repeated.

'No!' 'Mana said fiercely. She looked appealingly at Felipe Peralta. 'What must be must be.'

The old man nodded.

'If we must fight, we'll fight right here,' she told Stanton, then turned again on Armijo. 'Pay the gold to the trader as he told you. It is this *yanqui*'s due. But you won't take back the Corona. You've come too late for that.'

The governor bristled again at her tone.

'This one should be taught where to keep her tongue,' he protested.

'She has the right to speak,' Stanton told him, anger flashing in him as well. 'She's my

252

wife.'

'You put it delicately.'

Stanton did not miss the insinuation.

'Wife, I said, you pompous, smirking bastard! We were married in Don Felipe's house by one of your own priests.'

The startled governor shot a glance at Peralta. The old don nodded again. Armijo's manner changed hastily.

'A thousand pardons, *Señora* Stanton,' he said earnestly. 'An inexcusable rudeness. And I'm afraid I interrupted you as well. Would you care to tell me why I can't, as you say, take back this grant?'

'No,' 'Mana answered haughtily. 'I don't want to tell you or anyone else. Particularly my husband. I wanted everything to remain as it was. At least until we were in our own house. But you leave me no choice.'

Armijo grasped the importance of what she was saying, but not its meaning.

'I'm afraid I don't understand.'

'I am the woman you say you are trying to protect.'

Stanton stared at her incredulously. So did Armijo. Standing there on clay-caked bare feet to which wisps of dry grass yet clung, she glared in regal defiance at the governor.

'You—you are Maria Ruíz?' he asked in disbelief.

'I am Maria Dolores y Jesús Romana Ruíz de Herrera, an espoused woman. My title to the Corona Grant passed by law to my husband the moment we were married. Not even God Almighty can take it from him now!'

Felipe Peralta came stiffly to his feet and crossed to stand paternally beside her.

'The baptismal record as well as the marriage is in Father Frederico's register at Taos Mission,' the old man said proudly. 'Her family, tragically long dead, were my friends and neighbors. She has been as close to me as my own child all of her life. She is the last of an old and proud line.'

Still shaking his head in disbelief Armijo turned to Stanton.

'You knew this and didn't see fit to tell me?' he asked accusingly.

'He knew me as 'Mana, a woman of the Utes,' 'Mana said quickly, before Stanton could arrange his thoughts to answer.

'Don Felipe, Chato, and now Jaime have helped to keep my secret. How could I have persuaded Don Felipe and Father Frederico and Chato to consent to our marriage except by showing them that if he loved me enough to marry me as a nameless Indian, he loved me enough for the Corona Grant?'

Stanton realized that she was now pleading to him for understanding. But he needed to know one thing above all others.

'Why, 'Mana—why?'

She turned, put her hands up on his shoulders, and looked earnestly into his face.

254

'For the same reason that you came home that first time from Santa Fe and slept with me and didn't tell me that you had bought the land I could do nothing with alone,' she answered shamelessly. 'I wanted you to want me as you believed me to be, not as I am. I wanted you to possess me as a woman, not as a way to possess the Corona.'

Tears were very near the surface and her lips were trembling. Stanton put his arms about her and kissed them.

'Later, when you gave it all to me as a wedding present,' she continued when he had freed her, 'how could I take that pleasure from you?'

'Then the little house in the canyon above the Cimarron—you were living there when the Utes brought me in from the raid on the wagon train.'

'I was born there, *querido*. I have lived there all my life, except when I was away to school in Taos and Santa Fe. When the last of my family died, Don Felipe and Abelardo's father and the Utes looked after me. Until you came. Jaime has been there. He knows. But he loves you enough, too, to say nothing until I thought the time was right.'

Stanton looked at the unfinished walls, within which the Utes still remained at ready, facing Armijo's *soldados*.

'Then this was all foolishness. My vanity.'

'No!' 'Mana protested, anguished. 'Don't

255

you understand? Maria Ruíz was nothing. Now I am 'Mana Stanton. It is a new beginning. Finish those walls. Finish them quickly. I will love within them and live within them. When the time comes, I will die within their shelter.'

For the first time in his life, Spencer Stanton, a hard and disillusioned man with many other weaknesses, wept.

He had found his strength.

We hope you have enjoyed this Large Print book. Other Chivers Press or G.K. Hall & Co. Large Print books are available at your library or directly from the publishers.

For more information about current and forthcoming titles, please call or write, without obligation, to:

Chivers Press Limited
Windsor Bridge Road
Bath BA2 3AX
England
Tel. (01225) 335336

*OR*

G.K. Hall & Co.
P.O. Box 159
Thorndike, Maine 04986
USA
Tel. (800) 223–2336

All our Large Print titles are designed for easy reading, and all our books are made to last.